BEYOND REDEMPTION

ഊ Book One 03

Alex Hudson

ഊ03

First published in December 2019
Second edition published March 2020

ISBN: 9798620969678

My thanks to my husband, for the many hours of dedication to reading aloud to me, my work.

To my friend Jill for listening.
To my friends Pam and Arthur for being there, and to my other friends who know who they are.

My very special thanks goes to Diny van Kleeff who came to my rescue and Production Edited my novel.

Dedicated to my mother Beryl,
who I miss very much

PROLOGUE

Georgian England, 1787

Isabella was hurrying to get back home to the large town house in Berkeley Street when just down the road a commotion began.

A young thief ran past her, he was being chased by the watchmen, who the shopkeepers paid to safeguard their wares. In their haste to catch him, two watchmen roughly pushed Isabella out of the way and as they shoved her body hard against the wall, she fell to her knees in pain and horror, fearing for the unborn child, growing inside her. The child that as yet, Robert knew nothing about.

The fingersmith had taken refuge inside the Chandler's shop then, once he had seen the watchmen run past, moved out into the street again and seeing the woman who had fallen to her knees, rushed to her side.

When Isabella realised with relief that no actual harm had been done to her unborn child, she was able to get to her feet, with the aid of this seemingly kind passer-by.

'Are yer hurt, missus?' he enquired as he eyed up her bag, looking for a money purse that he might be able to acquire for himself.

'No, there's no harm done. Thank you,' Isabella said with gratitude, 'just the wind knocked out of my sails.'

'These little devils, out for a quick shilling, missus. But 'tis a tough life right enough,' he said as he put out his hand and lingered hoping she would take the hint. She brought out some coins from her pocket and handed them over.

'I'm sorry that's all I have on me.'

He quickly took the proffered money and with a tug of his forelock was on his way.

Isabella managed to continue on her journey, it was not good weather to be out in. The dark clouds were low hanging and the leaden skies spewed out a torrent of rain as she continued to push her way through the throng of street vendors who were trying to rid themselves of the last of their wares to anyone still out wanting to haggle for a late bargain. They were braving the weather but blocking her progress.

''Ere, love, I only have two of me gingerbreads left. Buy 'em love and let a gal get home and out of this bloody awful wefer, would yer?' came the cockney tones of a wet and bedraggled cake seller who had pushed herself in front of Isabella.

'Oh dear. I am so sorry I cannot stop, I'm in a great need of hurrying,' she politely called out over her shoulder as she hastened on her way.

Isabella loved the hustle and bustle of these squalid London streets which seemed more crowded than ever on this wet and miserable day.

The river Thames was close by with its muddy tidal waters snaking their way around the city, constantly being used for anything and everything, from the washing of clothes to the disposal of waste, human or otherwise. It was always busily heaving with all manner of vessels transporting its passengers to their destinations.

It was an excitement to Isabella, when the heavily laden ships arrived carrying their much-treasured supplies, such as silk cloth and French perfumes directly into England's foul-smelling capital. She was conscious that she was late and had to move more quickly to get back to the house that was owned by the wealthy Robert Bloom. Her home and workplace for the past two years.

She was now seventeen, slender and blessed with her late mother's brown eyes and dark hair. Isabella secretly considered herself Robert's intended for she felt sure it would become so in the near future. He was giving her a place to live, safe from all that town life might throw at a young girl who had been raised in the English countryside.

Isabella knew exactly how her living in this palatial house in the better part of London had come about. It had been an unwelcome necessity at the time, but she now considered it a gift, albeit unwittingly bestowed upon her by her own dear father's inexperience and misfortune. She understood that her father, Thomas Walker, had been forced into making a legal contract with Mr Bloom, which had meant she had to leave the grand estate where she had been brought up.

Isabella, having been caught up in the downpour of rain, was sodden through, her clothes were sticking uncomfortably to her body and her thick hair was clinging to her head. She was late and behind time for whilst out shopping for Robert's dinner she had met up with her friend Barbara Newman. She had spent too long helping her friend choose fabrics for the gown the dressmaker was to make for Barbara's well-rounded figure.

The two had become great friends, ever since the day, many months ago, when Isabella had helped Barbara as she stumbled in the street. Being a gentlewoman, Barbara should have had her maid with her, but she preferred to be free from the encumbrance of a girl to carry her purchases and usually had them sent on. Isabella liked her a lot; she was a lovely woman. She had auburn hair that she wore in ringlets, a cheery smile and was fun to be with. She was generous too, not just in a monetary sense but was also generous of spirit and she knew many influential people, being the owner of a successful gaming house that ran a side-line in female company. These were the businesses that kept Barbara independently well off, as she had no allowance from her wealthy father. Being head strong she had, to her regret, fallen out with him years earlier. So now she was able to stand on her own two feet and make her own way in life. She was a strong, confident woman who had a comfortable life and also, just as importantly, was extremely well-informed about people and their doings in the city and beyond.

When the shopping was done Barbara had asked Isabella to join her at the local coffee house. Although in a hurry, Isabella found it hard to resist.

Isabella loved the coffee house and Barbara was always greeted warmly if not discreetly by Molly, who was, for all intents and purposes, the owner. Only Molly, Barbara and her lawyer husband, Charles, knew that the legal owner was in fact Barbara herself but it suited all very well to keep the pretence.

The coffee house was a place usually only frequented by gentleman and not considered suitable for a lady, but Barbara's presence was easily accepted and ignored by the other patrons as most of them were her clients in one or other of her businesses.

Molly's Coffee House had become the two friend's usual haunt to pass away some time together. Charles, who was slightly acquainted with Bloom, recognised that he would dislike any tittle tattle that may pass between the two women and had advised that they keep their liaisons to themselves.

Although, in truth, Bloom couldn't care less. He was unaware of Isabella's education and felt no fear that any of his secrets would escape. The only interest Robert had for the gaming-house proprietor was what money he could rid her of.

Barbara, taking heed from her husband's words, had warned her friend not to disclose their companionship and, although a little puzzled, Isabella did as she was asked.

She found Barbara enjoyable to be with and was very fond of her mentor. Barbara knew things that others didn't and in a kind of way had taken over the role of mother figure from Mrs Price, the cook, back on the estate. Although she was sure that Alice Price could not teach her the ways of men or about London life as Barbara had done.

Barbara's guidance was invaluable to Isabella as she wanted to keep Robert's interest. She hoped that he would propose one day and make an "honest woman" of her. She had fallen in love with her master and had become tolerant of his demanding ways. Isabella was eager to tell her friend her news and so had readily accepted the offer of coffee.

As they entered the already bustling coffee house, Isabella's senses became alive with the aroma of the ground beans and the smoke-filled room of the other customer's tobacco habit as they sat in noisy conversations, huddled around their steaming coffee cups. The fire was crackling in the grate and Barbara led the way around the crowded room to a table as near as possible to the dancing flames, so that they could bask in its warmth on such a cold, wet day.

Molly looked up and on seeing them started to ready their usual order of coffee and baked buns, as they sat themselves down.

'Barbara, I have something to tell you. You mustn't tell anyone, promise me that you won't,' Isabella beamed as she placed a hand on her belly, which made Barbara guess immediately what her young friend was about to say.

'No, Isabella you can't be… I told you what you need to do,' Barbara said with worry as she lowered her voice and spoke in a hushed whisper. 'If he doesn't use an overcoat and you can't stop him at the crucial moment, then for goodness sake, wash yourself down there immediately with the solution of special herbs I gave you and drink the apothecary potion. How could you be so careless? He'll have you out on your ear, I'll wager.'

'Those potions and things haven't always worked for you, Barbara, have they?' Isabella retorted, a little hurt, 'and as for the overcoat, they are sheep's intestine and they are horrid. Robert hates them. Anyway, I love Robert and I know he'll do the honest thing, and we will be wed,' Isabella declared.

Barbara felt for the girl. She knew all about Mr Bloom and his ways. She often saw him in her gambling den along with his friends. Barbara knew that on some nights he preferred a night of whoring in the company of one of her girls named Mary, than to go home to Isabella. Mary had told Barbara that when truth was driven by alcohol he would confess to her some of his innermost thoughts and darkest of secrets and one of these confidences was that he would never allow himself to fall in love nor be tied down by any woman unless she had more money than he.

Robert Bloom could not and would not be in love with anyone but himself, Barbara sadly thought.

'Please don't be so sure that he will marry you,' she said to Isabella. 'Men are men after all, my darling,' she added, to help soften the harshness of her first words. She could not be cruel and mention the difference in their status and Isabella's lack of money. 'How far gone do you think you are?' she asked.

'About three months I think.'

'And how can you be so sure that you are with child?' said the older and more experienced woman.

'Well, I haven't had a bleed for over three months now and at the beginning, before I even suspected anything, I was unwell each morning. That has stopped now, thank goodness. I have seen all these signs before from the women on the estate back home,' Isabella explained. 'Oh. Barbara, don't be cross with me, he will marry me. I know he will.'

Just then Molly arrived at the table. 'Here you are, my dears. I've added a little something extra today, weather being so filthy,' she said in her usual friendly fashion as she put their coffee order and a good measure of rum onto the table.

'Thank you, Molly,' they said, welcoming the warming drink. Barbara poured the coffee and added the rum as Isabella put two clumps of the moist brown sugar into her cup and set about savouring the dark rich liquid.

'Very well, my darling, I hope for your sake he will, but if not, get word to me and I will help you.' The two friends then spoke of other things and had their usual enjoyable interlude.

When Isabella suddenly realised the time, she panicked, knowing that with bad weather like today, Robert could be home early and expect her to have everything prepared for the evening. This was not a good time to be out lazing away her hours and Robert would not be pleased with whatever excuse she gave. Isabella quickly bade farewell to Barbara and rushed out of the coffee house.

Her friend looked on after her with pity in her eyes. She tried to give advice as a parent would to her young friend for she knew that Isabella missed her father very much. Thomas still travelled to London every few weeks on estate business but he could only see his daughter every now and then when they could manage with the help of Barbara, to keep their liaison in secret, as Robert had forbidden their meeting as part of the cruel terms of the contract. Barbara knew that Thomas still spent time in the company of Mary. Although he had never entered her gambling house again and steered well clear of Robert and his friends.

Fortunately, due to her dear mother, Martha's schooling and Isabella's diligence to studying, father and daughter were able to communicate by way of letter and this Robert knew nothing about. Isabella was forever thankful to her late mother for that!

CHAPTER 1

Oxfordshire, 1769. Eighteen years earlier

Martha had to make an effort to keep up with her father, the Reverend Blake, as he walked briskly to the church where he was to give his usual Sunday morning sermon.

'Have you made answer to Lord and Lady Beaumont's wonderful offer of governess at Brayfield House?' he asked.

'I will be writing to them today, thanking them and confirming I will be with them soon, but it is such a long way to Wessex. I will miss you, Father.'

'I will miss you too my dear, but I'll be making visits to the Beaumonts and I will see you then,' he comforted.

As they entered the church by the west door, she contemplated how much her life was going to change.

After the service, back at the rectory, Martha set about writing to the Beaumonts.

'That young man is here again my dear,' her

father called up the stairs. She rushed to the window and there he was as usual, leaning against the wall opposite, looking at the house.

Martha had been introduced to him at a gathering some days earlier and he hadn't stop pestering her since.

He was visiting from London to negotiate a business deal with the Witney Mills to take their blankets to London, he had taken over the family business when his father had died.

Martha rather liked the young man at first, but he pursued her so relentlessly that he was now a nuisance. As a clergyman's daughter she would make visits around the village, but it seemed everywhere she went, he was there, declaring his intentions to marry her.

'Marry you, Sir. You hardly know me and moreover, I do not know you, Sir,' Martha would answer in exasperation at his impudence. She had this conversation with him time and time again and had told him that she was not interested in him.

* * *

Once the letter was written, she looked out of the window again and to her relief the young man had gone. Quickly, she put on her cloak, grabbed her bonnet and set out for the local coaching inn to post it and was shocked when he appeared again as if from nowhere.

'Good afternoon, Miss Blake. Pray, may I accompany you on your stroll?'

'Good afternoon, Sir,' she said stiffly, as there was no way to avoid him. 'I am taking this letter to the mail. In a short time I am to travel to Wessex to take up a governess position. It is a profession that I have dedicated my life to and there is no room for anything or anyone else. I am sorry to be so harsh in this matter, but you seem to have trouble understanding that I have no romantic inclinations toward you. Please leave me alone.'

But he had no regard for her plea and for the days that followed he did nothing but try to persuade her otherwise.

* * *

The night was darker than usual for the moon had been obscured by the clouds. Martha made her way home, having said her final 'goodbyes' before leaving for Wessex the very next day. With the darkness, came a quiet eeriness, but then the wind caught in the trees and she could hear the rustling of the leaves and the creaking of the boughs as it whistled and howled through their branches.

She had been detained and was much later than she had expected; she should not have been out so late this night. Feeling the cold she pulled her cloak tighter around her.

He appeared, suddenly, out of the darkness and tried to engage her in conversation but she turned away from his advances.

'Please leave me alone. I have told you before I am leaving Oxfordshire tomorrow. There is no room for you in my life.'

On hearing this he grabbed her by the arm and in his temper and frustration knocked her violently to the ground.

* * *

Moving to Brayfield House

The next morning, the Reverend Blake waved his daughter goodbye and the coach set off rattling along the cobbles to Wessex. Inside, Martha was relieved that she had not distressed her father by telling him of her ordeal the previous night. She had survived the wicked man's fists and his outburst of frustration. She had lain there in the dark and thanked God when she heard his footsteps walk away.

That dreadful man will not get the better of me. I am going to start a new life and fortunately I will not be seeing him ever again. She consoled herself as she nursed her bruises in silence.

After what seemed a never-ending journey the coach finally arrived at the inn close to her destination. As she alighted she saw a tall young man waiting with a carriage to take her to her the rest of the way. He walked towards her and introduced himself.

'Good afternoon. I'm Thomas Walker the Estate Manager at Brayfield House,' he said, 'Do I have the pleasure of addressing Miss Blake, the new governess?'

'Good afternoon, Mr Walker, Yes, I am Miss Blake.'

'Well in that case, welcome Miss Blake,' he smiled and proffered his hand. As they exchanged greetings she was glad this kind looking man was here to take her to the house, and she didn't feel quite so alone. Thomas directed Martha to the waiting carriage and they started the drive to the house.

As the Beaumonts imposing residence came into view Martha was taken aback by its grandeur. She wasn't expecting anything quite like this to be her home for the foreseeable future.

'What a magnificent house,' she exclaimed not being able to hold back her excitement.

'It is that, Miss Blake. I've been fortunate enough to live here all my life. The Beaumonts are good and fair masters. Anyone is lucky to be in their employ,' he said with pride.

The carriage pulled up at the side entrance and Thomas helped Martha down before taking her through the corridors to the main hall. She found it to be even more breathtakingly opulent with its marble floor, pillars and gilt-edged, plastered high ceiling. Paintings hung on the pale turquoise walls and beautifully embroidered, heavy drapes decorated the windows. She marvelled at it all.

'If you would like to follow the footman, he will show you to your room and I will have your belongings brought to you. Her ladyship suggests you rest after your long journey and she will meet with you tomorrow morning, before which, you will be introduced to the main members of the household staff who can be of assistance to you.' He paused then continued, 'I understand your father, the Reverend Blake, comes here quite often.'

'Yes, that is correct. I am hoping to see him during his visits,' she replied.

'Very well then. I will see you at eight of the

clock tomorrow morning, the footman will show you where to come.'

'Thank you,' Martha said with a small curtsy and Thomas gave a short bow from the waist.

Next morning at eight o'clock sharp, Martha descended the stairs to the kitchen and saw a line of people waiting to greet her.

Thomas stepped forward, 'Good morning, Miss Blake, let me introduce you to the staff. We are a friendly lot here and we help each other whenever necessary, we find it works better that way.'

Thomas then began the introductions, 'This is John Price, the butler, he is senior here on the domestic side of things,' Thomas indicated to John who gave a nod of his head and Mr Price took over the introductions of the next members of staff.

'Mrs Clara Grey the cook. Mrs Grey has been with us for several years now and keeps us all well fed. Is that not right Clara?' Mr Price said jovially.

'It is Mr Price. People can't work on empty bellies now can they?' Clara Grey said as she smiled at Martha and gave a quick nod of her head in acknowledgement.

'And this is Alice Price, my wife, we have been married for a good few months now. Alice is working as assistant to Mrs Grey.'

'Good morning, Miss Blake,' she said nervously

with a curtsy. Mr Price now moved swiftly down the line of the remaining household members.

'Well, that's it really. The rest of the servants you will get to know over time. Now if you are ready, I will take you to see her Ladyship,' Thomas said.

Martha realised, the position of governess gave her quite a high standing in the household.

* * *

Over the next couple of weeks Thomas made himself available for whenever Martha needed anything and she found herself becoming fond of him.

Thomas was a strong man who worked out in all weathers as the manager in charge of the entire estate. He was a good man, well respected by his workforce and greatly valued by his Lordship, Lord William Beaumont of Wessex, who was a faithful servant to His Majesty, King George III.

* * *

Thomas and Martha found that they could talk on many subjects and had much in common. They enjoyed each other's company and spent as much time as possible together. In fact the household staff believed them to be courting, as did the couple themselves. Even though they spent time together unchaperoned no one questioned their integrity.

However, when Martha discovered she was expecting a child she took Thomas into her confidence and he, wanting to do the right thing and to save her good name asked for her hand in marriage.

'May I have a word with you and her Ladyship, my lord?' Thomas requested and gave account of the situation.

'Yes Thomas, you and Martha are of course granted permission in the circumstances. What more can be done. Lady Beaumont and I, as you know, are in favour of marriages between the staff. It adds stability to the household.'

His lordship took care of the formalities with the Reverend Blake who was more than a little shocked with the news and his next visit was bought forward, due to the wedding needing to take place as soon as possible in the hope of stopping tongues from wagging. Martha was showing no signs of her condition and fortunately it was not uncommon for babies to be born earlier than expected, her Ladyship had explained, as a comfort to the young couple.

* * *

In the next few months that followed, many changes took place at the house.

Clara Grey's younger sister Jane's naval officer husband, Captain Morton, had recently died, leaving his wife a considerable fortune. However, Jane was unable to cope with losing her husband and, being of a delicate nature, came to Wessex to stay with Clara, who had asked and been granted permission to leave the estate so that she could go to live with Jane in Bristol.

The sound of her shoes clicking on the floor announced that Lady Beaumont had arrived in the anteroom just off the kitchen and called for Alice to come to her.

'As you know Alice, Clara Grey is to leave us here at Brayfield and you will take over in her stead. There will be a short period of adjustment, but I am assured by Grey that you will be more than able to perform the tasks required.'

'Yes, my lady,' Alice uttered nervously as she gave a quick curtsy.

'Don't worry Price you will do admirably,' she smiled and with another click-clicking of her shoes she was gone.

Although Clara knew that Alice was doing well enough as a cook, she doubted that she was ready to take her turn as midwife, as was the custom in these out of the way country estates.

'It looks to me that Martha Walker's baby is due almost any day now, Alice. It will stand you in good stead for future deliveries, being a first baby and all. You'll learn quick right enough,' Clara encouraged with conviction.

Alice smiled anxiously, so far it had been a responsibility that she had been able to avoid.

* * *

After a long and tiring labour Martha finally gave birth to a healthy baby girl, who she named Isabella. With the help of Clara, Alice was much relieved to have managed the duty she was dreading and felt a great accomplishment that mother and baby were doing rather well.

Clara was now able to pass all duties onto the new cook, leave Brayfield and live with her sister as planned.

* * *

Time passed quickly and as Isabella grew, she played with the Beaumont children and, although they were a bit older, she would join them in the schoolroom to receive the same tuition as they.

Thomas Walker was a happy man, he loved his wife and his young daughter. The position of estate manager had run in the Walker family for many generations, as he, Thomas was manager now, so was his father before him. He was saddened that the line would not be continued for as yet no other issues had been conceived.

'Anyone would think Thomas Walker that you love that job of yours more than me,' his wife Martha would tease.

'Never, my love, never,' was always Thomas' reply. Martha was the love of his life, but he did get great satisfaction from his work. One of Thomas' duties would take him away every few weeks throughout the year, when he was sent by his Lordship to London to deliver a pouch containing certain important documents. These documents bore the coat of arms of the sovereignty and his Lordship trusted only Thomas to deliver them safely, then bring the replying documents, if any, back to Wessex. He was always eager to see Martha and Isabella again on his return, even after only a few days away.

CHAPTER 2

Wessex, 1778. Nine years later

Martha lay in her bed, it was the fourth day that she had been confined to her room. Her eyes were closed, for to open them was too much effort. She could hear Thomas talking to the Beaumonts' physician. They didn't know she could hear them.

After nine years of marriage she still loved the sound of Thomas' voice, so calm and strong.

She was drifting in and out of sleep and couldn't make sense of what was dream and what was thought. Either way it was a comfort to her. She dreamed of how she tutored the local children in her Witney village and of her father.

Then, Martha was thrown into despair as she dreamt of the night before she left for Wessex. She remembered with horror how that man had brutally attacked her and knocked her to the ground. These thoughts made her whimper and she shivered. Thomas was holding her hand and talking to the doctor.

She heard their voices again,

'It's the fever,' the doctor proclaimed as he set about trying to treat her. He tried everything, from dry cupping to leeches. Finally, he shook his head.

'I doubt if there is any helping Mrs Walker,' he said. Then by way of an afterthought, 'I wonder if I could bleed her?'

This procedure was used often, but the letting of blood was not without risk. Thomas was hesitant, he had heard of cases where this had gone horribly wrong.

'I can think of nothing else, Thomas my friend. To put it bluntly, it's a case of do or die now I'm afraid,' the doctor whispered.

'You know I would want you to do all you can to save my Martha, but this...?' Thomas' trembling voice trailed off into despair as he reluctantly nodded his head in consent.

With haste the doctor selected the sharp Fleam from his bag, placed it to the vein in Martha's arm, struck it with the small metal rod and watched as the blood started to flow.

Unfortunately, some hours after the Fleam had been applied she still lay in a fevered state of unrest. The doctor made good the wound and picked up his bag to leave.

'That's it Thomas. It's up to Martha now,' were

his departing words.

As Thomas needed to resume his duties, he had to find someone else who could sit with his wife but no person could be spared from their work, so the task of sitting with Martha was to fall upon their eight-year-old daughter, Isabella. She was to sit with her mother and monitor her for any changes.

'Father, must I? I don't know what to do,' Isabella protested.

'I'm afraid you must Isabella. If there was someone else I wouldn't insist.'

Thomas knew this to be a difficult task for the young child, not knowing much about fevers and their consequences.

Lady Beaumont, who was fond of her governess had expressed a wish to take a turn watching over the sick woman to give Isabella a rest.

* * *

Alice sat and listened to Thomas' fears and concerns in the sitting room of the butler's quarters which was ideally situated just down the passage from the kitchen. Thomas gratefully accepted a much needed cup of tea with a good drop of the master's rum laced into it.

'For fortification purposes in these times of

trouble,' Alice had insisted. Tea, being an expensive commodity was usually kept under lock and key, so Alice would use the old tea grouts left over in the pot from upstairs and pour on more boiling water to make an extra cup or two for use in her sitting room.

Thomas looks all done in with the distress of it all, she thought.

'I have a great regard for Mrs Walker, and little Isabella is a delight,' Alice said in her local Wessex accent. 'I was there at Isabella's birth and I feel a great affection for the child as I do for you and her mother.'

'Yes, I know Alice. We are a family here,' Thomas replied. Even though there was a difference in status among the servants, it didn't seem to make any matter except when was necessary due to responsibilities and disciplines and this situation worked very well for all concerned.

'Now Thomas don't you fret, you go about your business, I will be here for Isabella to call upon if and when necessary. I'll make sure the child has something to eat and drink during her vigil,' Alice reassured the distraught man.

* * *

To help bring the fever down, Isabella was given a

bowl of cool water and a clean cloth to bathe her mother's burning forehead and a small dish with fresh well-water to dab on her mother's lips, in the hope that some might trickle its way down her parched throat.

Alice had impressed upon Isabella that should her mother stir or anything change in anyway, she was to fetch her at once.

'You will be fine Isabella my love. I'm only just down here, not too far away my lovely,' she said.

Isabella stood in her mother's dimly lit bedchamber, the small windows were pushed fully open. Martha's hair had been combed through and scooped high upon her head, but even this seemed to do little to aide her cooling down as her clean pillows were once again drenched in sweat.

She was covered by a thin white sheet and this too was now showing signs of the fever. Latterly, a bible had been placed by Martha's side.

Isabella stood diligently by the bed feeling awkward, she looked around the dark room and wished she could be somewhere else.

'Mother, please wake up. Mother open your eyes. Get up and we can go for a walk,' the little girl pleaded.

She pressed her tiny fingers into her patient's mouth with small droplets of water on them, in the hope that some water might actually stay in and not run out again down the side of her mother's mouth. A cup had proved useless.

Her fingers were so cold with the wet that they had become wrinkled and white and she could barely feel them.

Lady Beaumont entered the room, 'You go and have something to eat Isabella, I will sit with your mother. Take your time. I will be here.'

'Thank you Lady Beaumont' she said with a curtsy and ran off to find Mrs Price.

It was during one of Lady Beaumont's visits to Martha that she had stirred, half opened her eyes and spoke, albeit in difficult whispers to her Ladyship. Sadly, Isabella had missed this brief waking moment and Lady Beaumont thought it best not to mention it to the little girl.

* * *

After what seemed like several hours of devoted nursing, Isabella noticed the burning fever had left her mother's head and she was cooling down. Like a shot, she ran down the stairs, almost tripping as she went along the lower ground-floor passageway and into the warm kitchen,

'Mrs Price, Mrs Price. Mother is well again.'

On hearing this, Alice felt so relieved and exclaimed, 'Lord be praised.' She abandoned her duties as she quickly wiped her hands on her apron and hurried behind Isabella.

Upon entering the bedchamber, Alice's nostrils were instantly filled with the unmistakable heavy air and sour stench of a sick room. Realising, she quickly moved to the side of the bed.

'Stay where you are by the door Isabella, do you hear me?' she commanded. Alice touched Martha's face as she bent down to feel for any breath, just to make sure.

She then searched in her pockets for the two coins Lady Beaumont had given her to be used for this purpose and applied them to the dead woman's eyelids to keep them shut. She lifted up the top of the bed sheet and after muttering a few words to the Almighty, placed it over Martha's face.

The cook then walked over to close the windows and pull the hangings across the casement as a sign of respect. Isabella, who had been standing quite still watching in horror at all that was going on, ran and tried to pull the drapes open again shouting, 'No, no, what are you doing? She will wake up now, she has cooled down.'

Alice put her arms around the young child, 'No

my darling, Mother has gone to heaven now,' she soothed, 'Come with me and we will send for your father and Lady Beaumont.'

* * *

Martha had a simple service and the land manager's wife of nine years, was buried with the other members of the Walker family in the part of the churchyard that was set aside for the more senior of servants.

In the situation it had been decided that it was time for the Beaumont children to go to a school for boarding out, to continue with their education, but for Isabella, the academic side of her life had to cease.

* * *

Lady Beaumont asked her butler to send Alice to the morning room.

'Here Alice, Lady B's asking to see you in the morning room,' John, said to his wife as he came back into the kitchen.

'Oh! Good gracious John. The morning room? Do you know what it's about?' said the anxious cook, putting her hands to her cheeks.

'No I don't Alice, just make yourself tidy and get

up there to find out will you?' he urged.

Alice quickly took off her apron and cook's cap and rushed out of the kitchen, along the passageway to the servants' stairs that led to the family part of the house and through the door that led to the spacious corridor.

A little out of breath, she finally arrived outside the morning room.

She tucked away any strands of straying hair, took a deep breath and knocked on the oak panelled door. It was not usually her place to go through to "the family" part of the house, as her ladyship would usually meet with the cook in the room next to the kitchen to discuss menus and the like. A meeting in the morning room was most irregular and was throwing Alice into a dither.

'Come in,' her Ladyship called. Alice opened the door as quietly as she could and stepped just inside. Lady Beaumont was sitting at her writing desk and she saw Thomas was standing to the side of the room, next to the grey and white marble fireplace. The only sound to be heard was the loud ticking of the French clock that stood upon the mantle.

The room was so overpoweringly grand that Alice felt uncomfortable and out of place as she looked around at its plush velvet curtains. The carpet was deep and luxurious and it made her conscious that her comfy working shoes might soil it and make it dirty.

The large family paintings that decorated the walls were of people that Alice did not recognise, but she didn't have time to study them as Lady Beaumont addressed her cook.

'Mrs Price, close the door and come forward.'

The cook politely pushed the door softly closed. She turned the knob as gently as she could so as not to allow the door latch to make too much sound, she then edged herself shyly forward.

'I have been having a word with Walker here, regarding young Isabella and I have decided that in the situation it would be best for her to come and work in the kitchens alongside you with immediate effect. I'm sure it will prove to be the best solution for a while in the circumstance,' Lady Beaumont said with a smile.

'Yes my lady, thank you my lady,' Alice said nervously with a small curtsy as she started to back herself towards the door.

'Yes, thank you Price that will be all.'

Lady Beaumont now turned and looked towards her estate manager.

'Tomorrow, send Isabella to Mrs Price first thing. Now you are free to go about your duties Thomas.'

'I am so very grateful, thank you my lady,'

Thomas said, as he bowed his head and walked towards the already open door that Alice had fled through.

Alice scurried down the backstairs to the comfort of her warm, cosy kitchen. The fire was always lit in the hearth and the spit was turning slowly cooking a fine piece of meat for the evening meal, the aroma was inviting and mouth-watering.

Alice pulled out a chair and sat herself down at one end of the long kitchen table.

'John, it was about the child, the poor young thing, it's so sad, she reminds me so much of her mother it's almost uncanny. She's coming to work down here with me, I'll help her, give her a good bit of training,' Alice said with confidence.

'That's kind of her ladyship. I was wondering what was to become of Isabella. You know they really do look after us here at Brayfield, compared to some of the other estates hereabouts. To call you to the morning room was special circumstances indeed,' John admitted to his wife.

It was common knowledge that the Beaumont's had great empathy for the less fortunate and were known for the good treatment of their servants.

Isabella began work in the kitchen, alongside the other kitchen maids, under the watchful eye of Mrs Price. Alice enjoyed teaching her young charge the necessary skills to becoming a good and capable cook.

At the beginning, every now and then, the cook noticed that the little girl had neglected her duties and would find her at the back of the scullery crying for her mother. Alice could not scold the child as her heart went out to her; instead she would put her arms around her to try to comfort her.

As Isabella was growing up, any time she had spare, would find her in the schoolroom, with its familiar smell of learning that she loved so much. It had a strong, heady smell which came from the aged books and the ink spills on the wood of the desks.

She would sit in her usual seat and sometimes read the books from the tall wooden bookcase. She looked at the large oak desk at the front of the room and pictured her mother sitting there, teaching her students. Isabella, loved the hollow echoing sound of the schoolroom. She had tried to follow the curriculum of study her mother had set for the children, but it was a lonely task.

In those seven years that followed her mother's passing, Isabella, or Bella as she was now known in the kitchens, managed to improve her situation and was given duties by the housekeeper. Bella grew evermore into a capable young woman.

CHAPTER 3

Robert Bloom

Robert Bloom was a successful importer and exporter of commodities and a busy man. He had offices at the wharf and was forever waiting for ships to dock with the next consignment of cargo arriving from abroad.

He kept a watchful eye on the day-to-day handling of these shipments. He liked to show his presence to make sure Benson, his clerk who worked in the large, but gloomy offices, and Jack his foreman were doing the jobs they were being paid to do and not idling their time away.

The docks were busy, noisy places, with men sweating, tired and bad-tempered. The air was thick with cursing as the heavily laden ships were being unburdened of their precious cargo. There was the constant babbling of porters transferring the goods, noisy cranes, pulleys and other machinery, all squeaking and grinding in loud unison. There were horses and carts clattering up and down the cobbles of the quayside. The noise and commotion in the docks was deafening.

Arrogant customs officers with papers in hand poked into nearly every consignment, not wanting to miss anything that might escape duty. Robert knew that these officers needed befriending, for not to do so would be to his folly. He would do all he could to gain advantage.

Dockhands were hired once the lighter-men had transferred the cargo to the wharf. The cargo might stay on the lighters for days before it could be dealt with, exposing it to all weathers. Groups of watchmen were employed to prevent the river pirates from getting their hands on the goods. With all this and more, Robert wanted to be there to ensure everything went as smoothly as possible.

* * *

London docks, 1787

As it was raining it was not the best of days to take delivery of a stock of silk from France, but Robert knew it had to be done and the quicker the better. The rain, apart from being an infernal nuisance to him, could cause serious damage to the merchandise if not organised properly. It had the added annoyance that it slowed everything and everyone down, a situation that he was not best pleased about. He had been at the docks most of the day and he had had enough.

'I'm leaving now, Jack. Get me a hackney as quick as you like,' Robert shouted over the noise to his man in charge, 'and get Benson to ensure that the order of cloth gets to the tailor's in good time. Put the rest of the stock into the warehouse and be swift in this weather. We will sort it out tomorrow, it's getting too late in the day. Make sure the night watchmen are here before you leave tonight. Are you clear on all that?'

'Yes, sir,' said an exasperated Jack, who having worked for Robert these past few years had become accustomed to his master's every wish and mood. Jack knew that Benson was a much easier man to deal with.

Robert, now tired, wet and cold, was eager to see Isabella. The home in which he lived was highly fashionable and he kept a small household. He prided himself that his housekeeper, Isabella, having been brought up in the English countryside, was naïve and pox free.

He knew she would have heated the water for his bath, for she would know on a lousy day like today he would demand a bath, a change of clothes and some good food on the table washed down with a bottle or two of wine. If he had no guests coming for dinner she usually shared the meal with him. He liked her to join him, then several glasses of wine later she would spend the night with him in his bedchamber.

* * *

Robert, having returned home to Berkeley Street, pushed open the large door to his town house and shouted, 'Isabella. I'm home, where are you? I hope you've got my tub ready for me, by God, I could do with it today. I'm drenched to the skin and mighty cold.'

Sarah, the house maid, quickly ran up the stairs from the kitchen and nervously approached Robert. 'Excuse me sir, Miss Isabella is out at the market place at the moment buying food, I believe she has been delayed by the weather, sir.' She gave a short bob of submission as she turned to leave.

'Confound it, girl,' he barked, as he looked at Sarah, who was not the prettiest of girls he had ever seen. She had had the misfortune of catching, yet surviving, the disfiguring disease and her face displayed the evidence of the smallpox.

'Where's my bath, girl?' Robert roared, as he felt greatly inconvenienced.

'The water is hot sir and the house boy, Bruce, is pouring it into your bath at this moment,' Sarah said with head bowed as she tried to hide her face from the master's glare.

'Good,' said Robert. 'I see you have been taught well by Miss Isabella.'

'Yes, sir,' she replied as she gave another quick curtsy, then hurried back to the kitchen.

Thank goodness I have been able to save Miss from the master's wrath, she told herself.

Sarah had liked Isabella instantly, when the young fifteen-year-old had first arrived in the household to take up her position as a housekeeper. Isabella had no side to her nature and didn't seem to see Sarah's blemishes.

When Isabella finally arrived at the house, she entered at the back using the mews entrance as usual and was relieved to see that Sarah had started the dinner earlier and all was under control.

'Oh thank you, Sarah. But what about the bath? Is Master Robert home yet?' she gabbled away with worry.

'Yes, miss, I told him that you were at the market buying food and you were delayed in the rain. He is in his bath now and didn't seem to mind that you weren't here, so don't worry.'

'Thank you, Sarah,' Isabella said again with a smile as she gave the housemaid a hug.

Yes, Sarah thought to herself, *I would do anything for you, Miss Isabella, really I would.*

Upstairs, Robert walked into his bedchamber, removed his clothes and eased his chilled limbs into the hot water, sank back, relaxed and basked in its comfort. As was his wont, he thought of the night ahead with Isabella and idly cast his mind back to when he had first met her father, Thomas, some years earlier.

* * *

It had all happened one evening when Robert had been trifling away some hours with his friend Henry Brookes at a local London inn. The two friends were bored and looking for some distraction when they came across Thomas, who had travelled to London on his master's business. It was obvious that Thomas was not a simpleton but working on a country estate had rendered him inexperienced and vulnerable to worldly ways. He was a quiet man and chose to keep himself to himself.

Having made their acquaintance, Thomas met up with them whenever he had to travel to London on estate business.

Over time, and with a little probing, more out of

fun and mischief than anything else, Robert learnt that he had a wife who had, bore him a daughter.

Thomas had resisted the allure of the ladies they deliberately put in his way and he prided himself that, although a little tempted, he remained a disciplined, loyal and faithful husband. They did, however, manage to whet his appetite for the gaming house.

After his wife had died and some years later, Thomas was eventually persuaded to take his comfort of a young whore named Mary, this Robert and his friend, Henry, had found to be great sport and got great satisfaction from their achievement.

Robert had asked Mary to learn as much as she could about Thomas, for he was intrigued by his character and reluctance to divulge much about his life and this had become a challenge and a new game for the two gentlemen.

Robert knew that during drunken nights with Mary, Thomas would loosen his tongue and she was to pass on any stories in exchange for a monetary reward. Mary knew that although her best benefactor was Barbara, her employer, it suited her to make an extra shilling or two on the side.

In truth Thomas never had much news to tell, only simple family matters, but this information became of great interest to Robert, especially when Mary relayed the fact that Thomas' late wife's name was Martha, who had been a governess and was the daughter of a clergyman from Oxfordshire. Thomas disclosed that his daughter's name was Isabella and was the image of her late mother.

This news shook Robert to his very core as all this information confirmed to him that this Martha was the one and the same Martha Blake, there was no mistake. She was the woman from his past whom he had met when visiting Oxfordshire, she was a beautiful young woman, a parson's daughter. He had fallen instantly, totally and insanely in love with her.

He had tried to court this young woman but she had rejected him cruelly. She would rather teach children than spend a life with him. This he would not and could not accept and never forgave or forgot her for that.

He was now filled with jealousy and resentment for Thomas, who had stolen her from him. So much so that he began to hatch himself a plan. He knew how much Thomas liked playing the tables at the gambling house, and that he was on a bad losing streak and his winnings were becoming less frequent. He owed money to his friends, other gamblers and the gaming house. Robert reassured him that it was just one of those things and that Lady Luck would be smiling on him again soon.

Robert made the kind offer to pay off Thomas' debts, encouraging him that this would leave him with only one creditor, Robert himself and it would be easier to pay off just the one debt rather than several at a time.

'It would help to keep you safe, my friend, from the unscrupulous men who might mean to threaten or injure you in the act of recovering their money,' Robert had advised.

Thomas had taken the offer up eagerly but still found the gambling tables hard to resist. He also needed money for Mary's comforts and services so more was added to the account.

Yes, Robert thought as he lay in his bath remembering it all and how at last he had reaped his revenge on the beautiful Martha and on Thomas, who had won her heart, her hand in marriage and moreover that marriage had been blessed with a child named Isabella.

But I, Robert Bloom was cunning enough to secure Isabella as my own, as my housekeeper. In this very house. In my house, he gloated. What an utter fool you were, Thomas. You played right into my hands, Robert thought and actually laughed out loud as he congratulated himself on how he had managed to orchestrate this event. Robert often thought of this occasion with self-pride. He had his Martha after all, in the guise of her daughter, Isabella.

Thomas Walker

For Thomas, these events plagued and haunted his mind in never-ending torture. Thoughts of guilt would enter his head at random, wherever he was. They entered his dreams as nightmares and his waking moments as torment whenever his mind made him remember.

Thomas, thought that he had found friendship and what appeared to be safety under the watchful eye of Robert and Henry, but a while after Robert had secured Thomas' loan, he had sent word that he wanted to meet with him, in his office at the docks. This request mystified Thomas, as it was not their usual venue. In fact, he had never been to the wharf before.

Thomas entered the offices rather apprehensively, wondering what the meeting was concerning. The office appeared empty but as he closed the door behind him he heard muffled voices coming from a room at the back. As he approached he saw Henry Brookes through the open door, sitting at the desk opposite Robert.

When Robert looked up and saw Thomas standing there he raised his voice to become more audible,

'Come in, Thomas, my friend, I need to have a word with you.'

'Good evening, Robert, Henry,' Thomas said with a nod of his head. Robert was not about to waste words and got immediately to the matter in hand; he had waited patiently these last long months and he'd wait no longer.

'I won't beat about the bush, Thomas, I'll get straight to the point. It's regarding your outstanding debt to me. I'm considering some investments and need all of the money that you are owing to me so that I can finance it,' he said. 'I want it all back now, at once. I'm sorry, but that's the way it is, my friend.'

Robert's voice had taken on a rather curt, superior air. Thomas was astonished, there had been no indication that this was coming and he felt the blood drain from his face. In fact, he had only that day in the coach, on the way to London, checked his accounts and tallied up the sum of his debt and was shocked by its amount. He had decided he would try to work out some way to make slightly larger repayments to reduce it.

He stood there in disbelief, he couldn't possibly afford to pay back all that money in one go.

For goodness sake, it amounts to a considerable sum and I'm only on an estate manager's wage. This will be impossible. What could I have been thinking to allow myself to get into so much debt? He thought anxiously.

'I'm sorry, Robert,' Thomas began, 'but I won't be able to repay you in one amount, I just don't have that sort of money. I will need to make small instalments over time. Can we sit down and work out a repayment schedule?'

Robert gave out a single laugh as he leaned back in his chair resting his feet, crossed-legged, upon his desk as he smoked one of his imported cigars.

'Look, Thomas I'm a business man, you know that. I can't give money away, you must see that. I would end up broke and on the streets. What would my associates think of me? I vow they would take me for a fool.' Then, after a short pause he added, 'Unless, Thomas, that is what you take me for already?' He snorted angrily. He took a long pull on his cigar, rolled it between his fingers and, as he exhaled, looked at it, slowly examining it with great satisfaction, totally content in Thomas' discomfort.

Then, as if a decision had been made, he slowly put down the cigar and reached for the heavy cudgel that was laying on the desk that Thomas had only just noticed.

'No, Robert, of course not, it's just that I can't repay you, just like that,' Thomas replied with uneasiness. He was trying to think quickly but could find no solution. He concluded Lord Beaumont's help was not an option.

'You do take me for a fool, Thomas. Damn it man, I'll have you in Newgate this very night that I will,' Robert retorted with venom in his voice as he slapped the rounded end of the cosh into the palm of his hand as a demonstration of menace.

'No please, Robert, have some mercy. We have known each other for years now; I'm only a land manager. I won't let you down again, I swear.'

Thomas knew that Newgate was a grim place, a debtor's prison, amongst other things. It was inhuman, overcrowded, corrupt and dangerous. He knew that several inmates died each week from some terrible disease or often at the brutal hands of other prisoners. Thomas was not a weak-minded man but this was pushing him to the end of his tether.

To his surprise Robert's tone softened slightly as he put the cosh back down onto the desk. 'Quid pro quo, Thomas, you must have something to sell down there on that country estate of yours. Some horses perhaps that his Lordship won't miss?' he said dispassionately, as he removed a stray piece of tobacco leaf from his lips and flicked it onto the floor.

'No, Robert. I have nothing,' he said, gesturing

with his hands palm side up.

'Nothing? You must have something that you prize, man. Now tell me. What is it?' Robert demanded.

'No, nothing of any monitory value, sir, I swear.' Thomas' mind was racing; he had known Robert for a good few years now, but when it came right down to it, the number of evenings they had spent drinking and gambling together didn't amount to very many, in fact Thomas realised that his knowledge of Robert and his friend was very little.

'Very well, Thomas. What do you have of any value to you? Something you would give your life for.'

'Sir, I wouldn't give my life for any money and I can't go to debtor's prison, I have my daughter to think of. What would become of her without me working for Lord Beaumont?' Thomas was in despair and due to the nature of his job he was a strong man and on the verge of a brawl with this blackguard, who, it appeared, had turned tail on him.

'Well, then that's it, Thomas, that is the answer, right there in front of you, the answer to your plight, it's quite simple is it not? I'm in need of a new housekeeper so it would serve us both well for you to send your daughter to me. She can be my housekeeper and after a few years, why, your debt will be paid in full. How old is she now, maybe fifteen or so? So there we have it, man, get your daughter to me as soon as you like, if not sooner.' He laughed. 'Or, I am afraid, it is debtor's prison for you, my good man.'

Robert sneered. The job was done and he mentally thanked Mary for having given him all the information that he needed to make Thomas play right into his hands.

'What did you say, sir? My daughter? You dirty blackguard! How dare you? You're not fit to speak her name,' Thomas' temper was up and he yelled with his trembling fist clenched and raised high, ready to strike.

'Now, Thomas, don't be a fool,' Henry Brookes quickly shouted as he jumped to his feet and took hold of the distraught man's fists to prevent him from striking.

'That would get you in more trouble than in a debtor's prison, I'll be bound. Be sensible.' Henry guided his raised arm and lowered it to Thomas' side. He then gently placed a hand on his shoulder in a way to comfort the distressed man.

'Keep your temper, man. Be sensible, my friend,' he soothed. Thomas realised that Henry was advising some truth. He unclenched his fist. He was a broken man. *What a foolhardy man I have been. Martha would never have forgiven me to have acted in this way. This can't be happening to me and my Isabella.*

'Look, your debt is far too big for you to pay it off. So I'm suggesting this to help you, my friend. I run a small household and I won't have to pay a housekeeper's wage. This saving will help with my venture,' said Robert trying to sound sympathetic and reasonable, 'and your debt will be cleared. We will do it properly, legally if you will. I'll look after your girl for you, I'll see her right. She will have bed and board in a good part of London and for a young girl, why, what more could she want? I will make sure she is dressed well and maybe I'll find her some rich suitor, who knows? I will keep my eye on things. You have my word, Thomas.'

'But my daughter is so young,' Thomas said, distraught.

'I'm trying to help you here, Thomas. She will do well enough.'

Henry spoke again. 'He is right, Thomas, my friend. It's the only way. You owe too much money, you couldn't possibly pay it off in your lifetime. Your slate will be wiped clean. It's a considerable offer, my friend.'

Thomas knew that every word Henry was saying made sense. He was right. It was the only way. Defeated, he slumped back against the wall and reluctantly agreed.

How am I going to tell Isabella of my betrayal and how will I manage to persuade his Lordship into giving his permission to allow her to go to live in London?

Whilst all these things were going through Thomas' mind, Robert wasted no time and quickly finished writing the agreement that he had previously started in readiness for Thomas to sign and Henry to witness.

The next day Thomas was on his way back to Brayfield House. He had spent a sleepless night, even Mary couldn't console him.

As he travelled in the uncomfortable carriage, he worried himself into a restless slumber, going over the events of the previous evening, agitated about how he was going to explain all this to Isabella.

Would she ever understand and forgive him? How was he going to manage to second Isabella from Brayfield and get her to London? Around and around these thoughts kept tumbling through his mind as they had the previous night.

By the time the carriage approached the coaching inn for the final change of horses and to allow the passengers to take some rest, Thomas had come up with a solution, a little dubious, he knew, but he couldn't think of a better ruse that might satisfy Lord Beaumont. Thomas was an honest man and hated the fact that he had to deceive his Lordship as well as his daughter. Taking a little refreshment for himself he was obliged to make small talk with the other passengers. After making himself more comfortable for the last part of the journey, he climbed back on board and rethought his plans for the rest of the way.

Finally, the coach stopped outside the iron gates of the estate for Thomas to walk the mile long drive and into the house, up the servants' stairs and into the part of the house that he shared with his daughter. Although it was late, Thomas wanted to speak to Isabella as soon as he could as he could bear the guilt and shame no longer.

He knocked gently on Isabella's door, 'Isabella, are you awake? Can I come in,' he quietly called.

Isabella, who had been waiting for her father's return, called out to him,

'Yes Father, I am awake.'

Thomas opened the door and sat on the side of his daughter's bed.

'Isabella, I have something important to tell you,' he paused, uncomfortable in the lies he was about to tell. 'On my travels to London I chanced upon an old friend, who told me of a wealthy businessman who was looking for a housekeeper.' He paused again, not wanting to speak the words. 'I thought it would be a good way to get you into London's society and maybe get yourself a good suitor. You can't stay here all your life. Who are you likely to make a good match with? You don't even get to go out to the village very often. I have thought about this long and hard and feel that this is an opportunity that cannot be missed. Yes, my sweet, London would mean a very good start for you,' he gabbled out quickly. Thomas hated himself for being so dishonest with his daughter.

At this late hour and half asleep, Isabella tried to digest her father's words and when she understood them, she was wide awake and alarmed.

'Oh no, Father. No, I can't leave you and Mrs Price. No, Father. Please. I am very happy here. Thank you for thinking of me, Father, but I'd rather stay here with the people I know and mother is here in this house, in the schoolroom and everywhere,' Isabella exclaimed.

Thomas, in his guilt and panic, began to show anger, 'You have to go, Isabella, do you hear me, child? You have to go and there is nothing further to be said; it is all arranged,' he stated in a raised voice.

Isabella, unaccustomed to Thomas' annoyance, began to weep. He knew she had never heard him raise his voice in such a manner before. He began to despise himself. He was being so cruel to speak to his beloved daughter in this way. She had done nothing wrong. He had got them into this Godforsaken mess and she was having to pay the price for him. He felt so ashamed.

'Oh, my poor sweet child,' Thomas said as he gathered his daughter up into his arms. 'Isabella, what have I done?' A tear began to run down his cheek.

'Father, what is it? What's wrong?' she cried as she pushed her father away so that she could look into his eyes. Thomas' conscience could not keep up this pretence; he had to tell his daughter the truth. Full of shame, he explained how he and he alone had got them into this dreadful situation, how he had foolishly gambled away, what in truth, was another man's money.

Thomas didn't want to tell Isabella how much he loathed Robert for the way he had coerced him into the situation, for he knew that his precious child had to spend some part, at least of her life under this man's roof and she mustn't think badly of him, as it would make her life in London even more intolerable.

Isabella listened to the sorry story and thankfully was mature enough to know that there seemed to be no other answer, except perhaps, she suggested, 'We could ask Lord Beaumont for help.'

Thomas explained to her that Lord Beaumont would not be too kindly disposed to learn that his estate manager could be sent to debtor's prison due to his lack of self-control and it would still be impossible to repay such a large loan whoever he owed it to.

Isabella sat and held her father's hand. She spoke of her dear mother and knew that she had to protect her father, as he had protected her all these years of her growing up. Even though Isabella knew this was not what she wanted, there seemed to be no other way. She reluctantly gave her agreement, which was much to her father's relief.

To get his Lordship's permission to release Isabella from service, the pair had to concoct a story to tell. Thomas told his daughter of the idea that had come to him during his journey. He would invent a letter that had been sent to him by his elderly sister, telling how she had become very frail and infirmed. Thomas would ask for Isabella to be able to go and tend to her aunt in London. They knew his Lordship was a reasonable and kindly man. They trusted that he would allow this arrangement to take place. Thomas told her that was all he could think up.

Thomas went to his room but could not sleep. He sat with his head in his hands, his mind filled with thoughts of his wife Martha and how he had let her down in the worst possible way.

Isabella, full of misery, quietly cried herself to

sleep; she didn't want her father to hear to add to his distress. She understood her father was suffering as much as she, but he had the guilt and shame to compound his heartache. She loved her father dearly and she knew that he loved her. Isabella was intelligent enough to realise what her father had said was true about her finding a suitor and she would have a better chance to make a good match away from her sanctuary on the Beaumonts' estate.

* * *

The day Isabella was to leave for London, Alice was distraught. Her little Bella leaving was almost too much for her to bear. Alice and John hadn't been blessed with children so Bella become like their own.

'John, I must be brave for my Bella. It can't be easy for her to leave here. She looks nervous, poor little mite, but she has a job to do with looking after her aunt and we mustn't make it more difficult for her,' Alice quietly sobbed.

'Yes, my love' said John Price with tears in his eyes as he put his arm around his wife, but words failed him to console her any further.

Isabella put on her bravest face as she said her goodbyes, giving the biggest of hugs to Mrs Price and then her father.

'Please don't worry, Father,' she whispered.

'I will repay your debt for you. I don't mind, really I don't.'

'Isabella, don't go. I can't let you. . .' He wasn't able to finish his words as Isabella put a finger to her father lips and whispered, 'Father, I love you.'

As they all followed her outside Isabella was determined not to cry, she had an obligation and there was work to be done.

'I will write soonest,' she called as she hurried into the waiting carriage and it slowly moved off down the drive.

John Price was just able to choke out 'God Speed,' as he waved her goodbye.

Thomas turned away with his hand to his head. What have I done? He thought with anguish.

Thomas had asked to travel with Isabella as chaperon on her first journey off the estate, but his Lordship could not allow his land manger to leave his duties at this particularly busy time. So Thomas had asked the stage coachman, who he had befriended over the years of travelling to London, to act as protector to his daughter on the journey and for a small fee the coachman readily agreed.

Only when Isabella was safe in the carriage with

Baines, who was to take her to the coach bound for London, did she breakdown and cry tears of despair. Baines promised her his secrecy to her misery.

CHAPTER 4

All that was two years ago now and as Robert stepped out of the bath he looked at his strong physique in the mirror. *Yes, I am a fine figure of a man and any woman would be lucky to have me*, he told himself as he walked over to the door and opened it.

'Boy', he bellowed, 'bring me my brandy.'

Bruce had been ready, waiting for the sound of his master's usual demand. When he heard him shouting he climbed the stairs as steadily as he could, balancing a tray with the favoured crystal glass and a small decanter filled with some of the prized cognac that had been smuggled in from France, hidden in a cargo of silk.

Robert poured himself a drink then dressed himself in a white ruffled shirt. He ran the back of his fingers down the sleeve and delighted in its luxury. He pulled on close-fitting breeches over his silk-stockinged legs and put on a brocade waistcoat. As he was at home this evening, he wore his burgundy informal coat. His dark hair he wore loosely tied with a burgundy ribbon holding it in place.

Robert loved his clothes as they illustrated his opulence and success. It made him feel important, as well as showing off his physique to its best advantage. He again admired his own reflection in the mirror and thought of the night ahead with the beautiful Isabella as he felt and saw his excitement rise.

Robert felt smug that he was a very clever man to have acquired Isabella. In fact, he was delighted, as he knew he was the envy of all his friends having such an attractive housekeeper under his roof and in his bed.

Downstairs, Isabella was now quite dry from her trip abroad in the rain. She had changed into one of her most fetching dresses, over which she wore a blue bodice, showing what bosom she had to the best advantage. She had been able to discard her black servants' dress some time ago as Robert allowed her to look her most attractive.

'Oh! You do look lovely, miss,' Sarah remarked. 'Now, don't go getting yourself all messed up down here in the kitchen,' she added.

Isabella wanted the evening to go well as she was to tell Robert tonight of their wonderful forthcoming event. Again, she placed the palm of her hand against her abdomen, which had become a habit of hers when she thought of the child growing inside her. This act of anticipated motherhood was not missed by Sarah, who was filled with concern for her mistress. Sarah knew the master well enough to know that this was probably not a good happening.

Isabella caught the look of questioning that had turned to worry on Sarah's face and whispered with her finger pressed against her lips, 'Yes, you have guessed correctly, please don't tell anyone, Sarah, I'm telling Robert tonight. Oh, I am so happy.'

'I won't tell, miss, you can trust me,' Sarah replied as Isabella rushed over to hug the girl and let her share in the happiness.

Isabella climbed the stairs from the kitchen and walked into the library to sit and wait for Robert. She loved the library and was so pleased when she had first arrived at the house to see that Robert had so many books. It reminded her of the schoolroom and her mother. She would often avail herself of the beautifully leather-bound words.

Robert, however, had no idea that Isabella could read. Sarah warned Isabella against letting the master know and Isabella, although not understanding why, was always happy to take advice, so she kept this information from him. As it turned out, it was extremely fortunate that she had listened to Sarah because it was easier for Isabella to write to her father without Robert suspecting. Bruce would always collect the post and hand it to Isabella so the letters from Thomas went undetected by the master.

When Robert was either out on business or on one of his many social evenings, Isabella would invite Sarah into the library and teach her to read. They both took great joy in their shared interest in all manner of literature. Isabella was also wise enough to take a book of illustrations from the shelf, just in case Robert returned unexpectedly and she could busy herself turning the pages of the pictured volume.

Robert told Isabella very little of his business transactions or of the many ventures that were going on in his life. Believing that his servants were uneducated, he made the mistake of leaving various documents lying around, feeling safe in the knowledge that they could not decipher them. With encouragement from Barbara, although a little underhand, Isabella would steal a look and this was a way for Isabella to be able to be kept informed of the goings on in her loved one's life.

As Isabella sat and waited for Robert to ready himself, she rehearsed in her mind exactly how she was going to tell him her news. She prayed she would get the reaction she was hoping for and that reaction would be marriage.

Well, why wouldn't he, we are married in everything but name, she told herself.

She relaxed in the large velvet chair, closed her eyes and reminisced over the events of the last two years. Her mind drifted back to thoughts of her lonely and terrifying journey to London. She hadn't been very far afield before that day, as she had been under the strict and safe charge of Mrs Price at Brayfield. She remembered how her father had given her a necklace with a lock of her mother's hair in one side and a lock of her own baby curls in the other. He also gave her a little blue reticule; a small bag, which had belonged to her mother.

"Mother is with you my love, all will be well," he told her.

Whilst on the journey she remembered how she had felt close to her mother, who herself, had travelled from Oxfordshire to Wessex to take up her position on the Beaumont's Estate. It must have been difficult for her mother to leave her own father.

It was almost like history repeating itself she had thought and took great strength in doing as her mother had done years before when she was embarking on a brand new life.

Isabella's journey had been long and difficult in more ways than one. Her travelling companions were a mixed group. There were a couple of aged spinster sisters, Lizbeth and Lydia Collins, to whom the coachman had entrusted Isabella's safe keeping for the journey.

There was a ruddy faced man who was a farmer travelling with his wife. An elderly gentleman, who had the most atrocious cold and when he was not sneezing over everyone in the tight confines of the carriage, would be blowing into a large, fraying handkerchief.

Isabella was squeezed beside one of the elderly spinsters, but was fortunate enough to have a window seat to help take her mind out of the coach and into the surrounding countryside; it also enabled her to turn her head away from the elderly gentleman every time a new wave of sneezing took hold of him, as he was sitting almost opposite her.

Lizbeth and Lydia were both nervous travellers, or so they had it believed. They were going to London to visit their cousin. Lizbeth was busy trying to crane her neck around Isabella, to see out of the window.

"I am in fear of John Austin, the notorious highway man," she explained. Even when the kindly farmer reassured the ladies that the scoundrel didn't travel on this road, as it was the Portsmouth Road he favoured, she still insisted on taking the occasion to steel a peek, just in case she was able to catch a glimpse of the galloping horse, carrying a slender gentleman in the tricorn hat and tight fitting breaches, 'brandishing a pistol or maybe two!' she excitedly exclaimed.

It seemed to all who travelled therein that Lizbeth was in great need to set eyes on John Austin rather than the otherwise. Isabella liked the sisters and found them to be of great entertainment once she had become accustomed to their sense of amusement and was able to join in their little pretences.

As the wind howled around the outer surrounds of the coach, Isabella tucked her cloak around her even closer. The passengers exchanged stories and Isabella explained with some pride that her father had been able to secure her the position of housekeeper to a wealthy London businessman.

Their journey was interrupted by the need to change horses at the various staging posts en route to London but they finally made rest for the night at a quaint coaching inn near Thatcham, where they were able to partake of a hearty meal before retiring for the night.

Isabella had the pleasure of sharing a room with the two sisters, who talked constantly of the highwayman who could be just outside their very doors to rob them of their belongings and maybe put his hands about their person whilst they slept that night.

Isabella however, could not join in their fun as she again began to feel the misery of her situation. She craved for the security of the Beaumonts' estate and Mrs Price with her comforting hot milk toddys that she would give to Isabella to help her to sleep on bad and stormy nights. She missed the sound of her father's footsteps in the corridor as he made his way to his bed in the room next to her own. Most of all, she missed her mother.

The sisters had paid extra for a fire to be built in their room and it gave off a warm glow to coat the walls in a comforting light as well as producing a certain amount of warmth. They slept in their clothes and Isabella brought the blue reticule into her bed with her, in case the sisters were right and a highwayman might steal her prized possessions.

Once she had quietly cried herself to sleep, she actually slept quite soundly and awoke next morning refreshed.

Things always look better in the morning she reminded herself of one of Mrs Price's famous sayings.

They ate a small breakfast and once they had made themselves comfortable for the rest of the journey they all boarded the coach, "For the next leg of the adventure," as Lydia excitedly put it.

When the jolting and jerking coach finally arrived

in London, it was about three thirty in the afternoon and Isabella had turned her thoughts around from total despair to that of slight excitement.

She alighted from the carriage, bade farewell to her fellow adventurers and assured the sisters that she was able to shift for herself now, she thanked them for their company during the journey.

She stood waiting alongside the coach and wondered what to do next, the box containing her belongings had been passed down from the coach and was sitting on the ground beside her.

As she looked at the scene that surrounded her, she saw and heard such a myriad of new sights and sounds. There were people milling around, in all shapes and sizes, in different ranks of society: the street traders crying out their wares, the infestation of ballad singers, broadsheet sellers and people just hurriedly going about their business. The noise was ear-splitting. The sounds of the printing presses or people hammering some metal or other. It seemed everywhere people were all talking and shouting at once. This general hubbub of city life had never been heard by Isabella before.

The stench was a disgusting mixture of dead fish and rotting vegetation of some sort or other. There was a decomposing cat lying near her in the road and waste running raw in the streets. Isabella saw many a fine lady or gentleman holding a lace handkerchief to their noses as they walked by, carefully picking their way around these obstacles. All these things were not commonplace to a country girl, and it made her head spin.

Father, you didn't prepare me for all this, she had thought.

She looked around at the overhanging houses; the narrow streets and the cobbled roadways under foot, with all manner of refuse strewn around them and she was confused as to what to do next.

A finely dressed, rather pleasant-looking gentleman with dark hair and of good appearance walked towards Isabella as he proffered his hand, to take her own trembling hand in his.

He had been waiting for her arrival and was eager to see her and so had taken it upon himself to greet her personally. He was so taken by her beauty and her likeness to her mother that he started to raise her hand to his lips but he remembered his position just in time.

'Why, I do believe you must be Isabella,' Robert said. 'I would know you anywhere you look so like...' Robert hesitated a moment then quickly corrected himself, 'your father,' he added, 'I am Robert Bloom and I would like to welcome you. You are here to work as housekeeper for me.'

Isabella felt a little shy at this rather formal introduction. He had a young face but was probably older than he looked, Isabella surmised. She had only been used to being treated like a child and now she was here in London as an adult.

'Yes, sir,' she replied with a little curtsy. Robert was enchanted by the girl and her looks.

I must be the one to remember her place in my household and not let her overstep the mark, he thought.

He ordered his man Jack, who had been standing just behind him, to gather Isabella's belongings and take them to the house, while he escorted his new housekeeper.

When Isabella saw the Bloom residence she was thrilled, for although it was much, much smaller than the big house in Wessex, it still had a look of grandeur about it that Isabella had been so afraid would be absent in this London dwelling.

Once inside the house she was introduced as Mrs Walker, which Isabella was rather pleased about, as the term 'Miss' was only used for very young girls or harlots at the point of introduction. The small number of staff had been assembled in a line in the main hall.

Robert called out the name 'Sarah' and beckoned her forward. 'Sarah is the parlour maid and cook, as we run a small household here,' he said.

Isabella recognised at once that the poor girl had suffered the smallpox as she held her head low.

'Hello, Sarah' Isabella said and smiled at her, showing she was unconcerned by the scars on Sarah's hands and face.

Robert moved down the line. 'This is Bruce, the house boy. He is not a resident here but comes in to work and help out each day. This is Jack, who you have already met at the coach and who has brought your belongings into the house. He is in charge of the men at the docks. He can be called upon to get you help, if you need him for any heavy work, just get word to Benson my clerk at the office and he will organise it. Sarah will show you what is necessary,' Robert continued.

Isabella was amused that Sarah gave a little curtsy, while Bruce and Jack gave a short bow from the waist as they all called her Mrs Walker. Sarah looked as if she was just a little older than Isabella. Bruce looked a good few years younger and Jack looked as if he was aged somewhere in his twenty's.

'Sarah, take Mrs Walker up to her room and show her around,' Robert instructed.

'Yes, sir.' Sarah bobbed with her reply and very politely asked Isabella to follow her.

She took Isabella up to the top-floor room which

was to become her own. It was a small room with a bed and a cabinet with drawers for her clothes; it had a tiny window with a small curtain that was pulled back to the side, to let in as much light as possible.

But it is big enough, Isabella thought to herself as she fingered her mother's locket around her neck.

* * *

Isabella carried out her duties as had been taught to her by Mrs Price and she had started teaching Sarah, all she knew about the art of cooking and housewifery. She knew that Robert was extremely pleased with the way his household was shaping up. He was always complimenting her on how he had never tasted such fine food and how the house was being run like clockwork.

Isabella loved her work; she particularly liked it when Robert had guests for dinner and she could concoct a special menu. She would serve the meal with the help of Bruce, who had to stay late on these occasions and so would sleep on the floor in the kitchen.

She was becoming fond of Mr Bloom and was attracted to his good looks. She felt happiest when he was at home and she could be near him. She also liked the power that he demonstrated, which was coupled with a sense of danger.

'Be careful,' Sarah had warned Isabella. 'I would hate to see you compromise yourself.'

Isabella was taken aback by this comment but she knew the girl meant no ill and accepted the warning without taking offence.

Isabella thought back to one particular day, after a few months had passed when she was called to the library to finalise the menu for that evening's dinner guests.

As they stood talking she felt the closeness of his body within inches of her own and she could smell the masculinity of him. Without realising Isabella started to lean very slightly in his direction, as if he was a magnet pulling her to him, their arms touched, but as he turned away toward the door at the sound of Bruce entering to replenish the fire, she couldn't hold her balance and she stumbled and nearly fell.

Robert looked at her, smiled and gave a chuckle, she recalled.

'Oh, Sarah. He knows how I feel,' Isabella told the maid, when she was safely back in the kitchen, 'He knows, Sarah. What am I to do? Oh, I want to die. How can I face him again?' wailed Isabella with embarrassment.

'But face him you must, miss. I'm sure it will be fine and he probably doesn't know anything of the kind,' Sarah consoled.

That night the dinner had gone well and Isabella was helping Sarah put away the cleaned plates and bowls, when they both heard Robert at the top of the kitchen stairs.

'Isabella,' he called 'I have to speak to you.' Sarah watched as Isabella put the drying cloth down and quickly ran up the stairs. Robert, having escorted his last guest out of the front door, was standing, leaning against the frame of the doorway to the drawing room, he held his brandy glass in his hand. She could see that he had had a good few glasses already.

'Come in, Isabella,' Robert had said as he held the door open with his free hand, which meant that she had to duck under his outstretched arm to enter the room. With what seemed like one movement Robert had closed the door behind her, taken her in his arms and as the brandy glass tumbled to the floor, he was kissing her full on the mouth.

Isabella had never felt anything quite as indescribably exciting as this before.

He pushed her against the closed door with the weight of his body and, as a surprised Isabella spontaneously moulded herself to his supple physique, she could feel his firmness pressing hard up against her; it gave her an unfamiliar amazing thrill. She had played games of kiss chase with the boys back on the estate but that was nothing like this, they were nothing like Robert.

He started kissing her neck and caressing her so eagerly that she didn't want him to stop. He breathlessly whispered, 'Oh Mar...' He was in enough control to just about realise his blunder before he whispered the full name of Martha. He corrected himself. 'Isabella, my love, I adore you so much.' Isabella let out an involuntary groan which excited Robert. Her breathing quickened as he bent his head and kissed her neck again. Then he was kissing her on the mouth with his tongue teasing, gently brushing her lips. She could not believe the feelings that were pulsing through her very being and she felt a desperate need for him, annoyed that her clothes were in the way.

He breathlessly spoke the words, 'Isabella I want you so much I can't keep myself from you, you are so beautiful.'

He quickly unbuttoned his breeches, then pulled up her skirts and slid his hand under her petticoats and gently caressed the top of her thigh. He put his knee between hers and gently eased them apart. Robert's searching fingers were eager to find her feminine place, his fingers were gently probing. Isabella's excitement was mounting to heights that she had never known before. She knew that she was wet down there as he said, 'I can feel you are ready for me, my love.'

'Yes, now Robert, now,' she begged. She had a need for him that was uncontrollable, so overwhelming, she could wait no longer. She ached with longing and excitement. In the next moment she felt him enter her moist, silky place. His frenzied hands behind her, he grabbed to pull her even closer toward him. As he pushed himself further towards her, he let out a moan of pure ecstasy, and she cried out in intense pleasure. Then she felt a short moment of a quick, dull pain that made her gasp, as she felt him push deeper.

He moved easily and fast, again and again. Their mingling sweat was trickling down their bodies. Their passions were mounting then he shouted out, 'I will love you forever, I promise'. He then gave one final long, hard, determined thrust, as he made several deep throaty grunts. She felt him shudder several times and his thrusting became very slow and then subsided as his whole body relaxed against hers.

'Oh, Robert, I will love you forever, too' she whispered, but he didn't seem to hear her. As he removed himself from her, she felt a warm trickle on the inside of her leg.

Robert was straightening his clothes and he was using the bottom of his shirt to clean himself. He vainly ran his hand through the strands of his wet hair that had struggled themselves free from its ribbon. Isabella was still spellbound in the moment of love and moved close to cling to him. He put his hands on each of her arms and held her away from him and said, 'Go and clean yourself, Isabella. You will find some blood this time but don't be alarmed, you won't bleed like that next time.'

Next time. He said, next time, she excitedly thought to herself and smiled. He took her face in his hands and gave her a quick kiss on the lips.

'Now, go to your room and don't tell anyone of this.'

Isabella had walked up the stairs to her room in an almost trance-like state. Her back felt sore from the pressure of being held so hard against the drawing-room door. She had often heard about a man and a woman lying together from the loose talk and giggles of the parlour maids back on the estate, but they didn't describe such pleasure in any of their horseplay.

Oh Robert. You said you would love me forever and you promised. Oh. Robert, I love you, too, she had smiled to herself.

She had fallen asleep that night so very contented

and happy. She recollected that she told herself that she was no longer a young girl, she had just become a woman, and was living with the man she loved, and he loved her. He had promised.

That was the last night that she had slept in the little attic room as she was moved into a bedchamber on the same floor as the master's. Her life had changed from then onwards.

Sarah and Bruce call me miss now, but that's until I'm Mrs Robert Bloom, she told herself.

Although she still carried out her usual duties, for appearances sake as Robert had insisted, she felt that she had a better standing in her lover's house, she was after all, for all intents and purposes, the mistress of the house now.

Yes, she remembered that first time nearly two years ago, with warm affection, and tonight was the night that she was to tell Robert of their baby and she would definitely soon become Mrs Bloom.

Robert having bathed and changed for the evening entered the library to relax with Isabella before dinner.

'You look enchanting, my love,' Robert said.

'Thank you, Robert, I must say you look very dashing yourself. We look a handsome couple, do we not?' Isabella replied, almost bursting to tell her lover her news. But she knew that she must wait until after the meal and then they wouldn't be interrupted.

Robert walked over to the little round table that held a silver tray on which sat a brandy decanter and glasses. He removed the stopper and poured two glasses of the good-quality liquid. Isabella had taken a liking for brandy and wine. She thought about Mrs Price, who would not approve, but this was London and things were different here.

Robert sat in his favourite leather chair opposite his lady and discussed his day; this had become their custom each evening when Robert was home. Although not given to disclosing much about his business, he chose on occasions to boast and today he told of the lighters that had been able to bring ashore some cloth that had arrived from France, which enabled him to obtain some cognac that had been hidden within the merchandise and thus saved him the tax duty that should have been paid to the government on his secret cargo.

He liked to show off and let Isabella know just how clever and devious he was, and Isabella showed how suitably impressed she was of his cunning.

Then Sarah was summoning them into dinner as the meal was about to be served. Isabella looked at the clock above the fireplace and was surprised that the time seemed to be going so slowly this evening. She longed for the moment when they would come back into the library or the drawing room, depending on Robert's whim, to tell him her news.

As they entered the dining room Isabella was pleased to see how well the table looked now that the candles had been lit and the selected bottle of wine to complement the meal had been opened and was ready for the pouring.

'Why, my love, you have supplied us with a real treat this evening,' Robert said, feeling rather pleased with the spread set before him.

'Yes, Robert. I thought we could have a special meal this evening,' Isabella said, not realising that Robert had misread the situation as a magical night of passion, but Isabella had different ideas as she wanted to mellow him before she imparted her news.

Once they had finished eating, Isabella could not wait to move to the comfort of one of the reception rooms.

'You seem rather agitated tonight, my love,' Robert observed as he pushed his chair back from the table and gestured his outstretched hand for her to leave her seat and accompany him.

Sarah entered the room to clear the table. Isabella had already told Sarah that once they had vacated the dining room they were not to be disturbed. Sarah knew the importance of tonight and she worried that it might not go as well as Isabella had expected.

Robert chose the drawing room to settle for the evening, and he asked Isabella if she would like a game of cards or maybe play some music on the harpsichord.

'Not tonight, Robert, if you please. I just want us to sit as I have something important to tell you.'

Robert turned and passed a brandy to Isabella. 'Something to tell me, my sweet? Pray tell, what have you on your mind?' Robert said calmly as he took a seat on the long upholstered sofa.

Something to tell me. What could be of any consequence in her little life? But listen, I will. He decided to indulge her.

Isabella took a large swallow of her drink and began to speak the words softly, but instead of telling her news as she had rehearsed, it all came rushing out in a hurry and not at all as she had intended.

'Robert, we are to have a baby, I am with child.' She couldn't contain herself and babbled on excitedly. 'Isn't that wonderful, Robert? Our child. You will marry me, Robert, won't you? But we will need to be quick before I begin to show,' she rushed on.

Robert looked at Isabella as he took a long swig of his brandy and then remained quiet while he contemplated the amber liquid in the glass. It seemed to

Isabella to be an absolute age as he thoughtfully digested the situation.

Why has he gone so quiet? What is he thinking? She wondered but remained silent.

He set down the glass and walked over to Isabella's side.

'My love. That is the best of news. Of course I will marry you if you bear my child. Now tell me how many months is our little one already?'

Isabella, her mind spinning with happiness answered, 'I am nearly three months on, so I think,' she smiled.

He took Isabella's hand and gestured her to stand, he then held her in his arms and kissed her passionately.

'You haven't told anybody yet have you, my sweet,' he said, worrying about his business as well as social reputation. There was still many a puritan view held by several of his older business acquaintances.

Isabella thought about Sarah. She hadn't really told her. Then there was Barbara who had also guessed. Isabella felt safe in the knowledge that she trusted their discretion implicitly.

Well, I hadn't actually told them, she thought as she hurried on.

'No, my love, I wanted you to be the first to be

told. I understand that we will have to be wed before we tell anyone about the baby. I would like my father to know of our plans to marry. I think that we should invite Lord and Lady Beaumont, they have been good to me over the years,' she rambled on excitedly. She had the wedding arrangements and the baby running through her mind all at once. In all her life she couldn't believe her happiness and good fortune. Then Robert said,

'Well, I was thinking that we shall have to go away and have a quiet wedding in secret and then come back and announce that we are married. It is quite fashionable here in London, you know. Now let's go to bed and celebrate our wondrous news.'

Isabella felt very disappointed. *A quiet wedding. I want to have my father with me. But then, I'm sure Robert knows best*, she trusted.

Once inside the bedchamber it was as if the news that he was to become a father had excited Robert beyond all measure, for he made love to her that night with the greatest gusto and passion, they were hot and sweating and he was far more energetic than she had ever known him to be, in fact he was a little rough. Then as always at the very moment that he made his final thrust he cried out, 'I will love you forever, I promise.'

Isabella exhausted by their lovemaking smiled and laughed as she patted her belly, thinking of the child that she was carrying.

The next morning Isabella awoke and found Robert sitting on the bed beside her, dressed and ready to go out.

'Now, Isabella. As exciting as our news is we must keep it our secret. No talk of weddings or children. We shall make our marriage our surprise, then tell everyone once we are wed. Then after a month or so we will announce the baby. Do you hear me?' he said with some urgency.

'But, Robert why? I understand about the baby but what about the wedding? Can't we just tell a few people?' Isabella said with great disappointment in her voice. She had dreamt about inviting Barbara and Sarah and having at least a little celebration.

'We must keep it as quiet as possible just in case we give ourselves away. It's fashionable, as I mentioned last night. This is how it must be, Isabella. I insist upon it, do you hear me?' he said again then, realising he had spoken a little too harshly, continued, 'If it pleases you, we will celebrate tonight just the two of us, a special night, I promise you my love.'

'Very well,' said Isabella, feeling quite upset, but she didn't want to annoy Robert, who might change his mind and not marry her after all, just as her friend Barbara had feared.

Robert kissed her on the forehead and walked to the door of the bedchamber, there he turned and smiled and uttered, 'Isabella, Isabella, Isabella,' as he shook his head.

She laughed and said, 'Robert, Robert, Robert' he laughed too and as he closed the door behind him rested a while upon it as he thought to himself. *She is such a sweet child.*

As Isabella got herself dressed she rehearsed the sound of her name: 'Isabella Bloom,' she said aloud. 'Mrs Robert Bloom,' she said again and laughed with joy as she made her way down to the kitchen to see Sarah.

Having taught Sarah much about running the house she no longer had to be in the kitchen quite so early these days. Sleeping with the master did have some privileges she smiled to herself and soon any day now she was to be his wife.

* * *

Robert, left the house and walked with great purpose along the London streets. *Now, I know it is here somewhere.* He managed to find the shop that he was looking for. It was situated next to the watchmaker's.

He entered the jeweller's shop, for he wanted to buy Isabella an exquisite piece of jewellery. He really wasn't at all sure why he felt so compelled to buy this gift. *But the girl deserved it after all said and done*, he told himself with a small feeling of guilt edging his mind, an emotion he was not accustomed to. Once inside the shop he found almost at once the piece that would make her happy. It was a gold brooch in the shape of a pretty little bow encrusted with diamonds and small red stones. She will love this, he thought.

Outside the shop with the brooch safely inside his pocket he headed to his next, most urgent, port of call.

CHAPTER 5

Sarah was clearing up after Robert's breakfast when Isabella entered the kitchen. She and Sarah had made it their custom to eat their morning meal together when Robert was not at home, so they sat down at the large kitchen table.

'Sarah, I know I can trust you not to speak of this to anyone and I will tell Barbara of course,' Isabella took a dramatic paused before she continued with excitement, 'My wonderful news is that Robert has asked me to marry him. It's going to be a quiet affair and we are going away together for the ceremony and we will keep it secret until we return as man and wife. Then, after a while, we will announce that we are going to have a baby. Oh. I'm so excited.'

Isabella was talking so fast she didn't seem to take a breath as she hurried on. 'We are having a little celebration tonight, just the two of us. Or should I say three,' she giggled as she put her hand on her belly for the umpteenth time.

'When Miss Isabella? When will the wedding

be?' Sarah questioned with some disbelief in her voice.

'Soon, very soon, Robert is making arrangements today I believe, as we have to be quick,' Isabella said excitedly.

'Oh Miss, I am so pleased for you. I didn't think anyone would tie the master down, really I didn't,' she said.

Isabella was a little shocked by this statement but chose not to pursue it, 'I want to make this a special night. We will be talking about our plans, so after the meal this evening will you make yourself scarce, Sarah, and please make sure we have no interruptions. I'm putting you in charge today.'

The day carried on almost as normal except Isabella was fit to bursting with her news. Robert surprised Isabella by returning home earlier than usual in readiness for the night ahead.

'Why, Robert, you are home so soon,' Isabella cried with joy.

'Yes, my love, I couldn't keep away. Now run and get yourself ready in one of those beautiful gowns of yours and we will start our merriment early,' he said.

Isabella disappeared into the first-floor bedchamber that had become her dressing room, and chose her favourite dress with the blue bodice that reminded her of their first night together.

As she readied herself she thought how happy her mother would have been, hearing about her forthcoming marriage to Robert and Isabella heard her mother's words in her head and felt the pang of loneliness that she often felt when her mother entered her mind. She would often try to picture her and wonder what advice she would have given to her young daughter. She thought at that moment how sad it was that her mother wouldn't know about the child that she was carrying.

If it is a girl I will call her Martha, she thought. *I will write and tell my father all the news once we are wed.*

Isabella pulled on her white stockings, slid her feet into her silk-buckled shoes and checked her reflection in the mirror. Sarah had already curled Isabella's hair and set it high upon her head with a large single ringlet which hung around her face and down onto her bosom. She put the red pomade stick to her lips. She was engaged to be married and tonight she wanted to look her best.

Isabella walked down the large staircase and seated herself in the library as was her custom as she waited for Robert.

* * *

Robert was in a hurry. He had washed in the bowl of hot water that had been brought to his dressing room by Bruce, made a quick change of clothes and was just draining his usual glass of brandy as he prepared himself for the evening before him. He took out the package that he had purchased earlier for Isabella and put it into the pocket of his silk waistcoat, and made his way down the stairs to meet her in the library to have their usual drink before dinner.

'Isabella, my own true love, how wonderful you look tonight. It must be that you are with child, my love,' Robert said, as he was genuinely shocked at how beautiful she looked. Isabella was so thrilled at Robert's words, as she never thought in her wildest dreams that she was soon to be Mrs Robert Bloom.

Robert poured a large brandy for them both and passed a glass to Isabella. He sat in his chair opposite her and drank in her beauty. She was so like her mother, he thought.

Sarah beat the gong and they entered the dining room.

'Oh. Robert I'm so in love and I'm so happy' Isabella whispered as she looked up at her intended.

'I am too, my love, I'm very fortunate indeed,' he whispered back as they took their seats at the table.

Robert dismissed Sarah and Bruce and said that

they could do any clearing away in the morning. Robert sat next to Isabella throughout the meal, instead of his usual place at the head of the table, and Isabella felt so loved. This was bliss indeed, she thought.

When the meal was over, Robert felt in his pocket for the present that he had bought earlier and gave it to her, she quickly opened the pretty wrappings and found inside the diamond-and-ruby brooch and immediately asked him to attach it to her gown. She felt a little upset that it wasn't the engagement ring that she had hoped for but understood it was a symbol of their secret.

He then poured them each another glass of wine and they played a game called "loser drinks down". A game that Robert played with some of his gambling friends for merriment. He would ask Isabella a question and if she got the answer wrong she had to drink the whole contents of her glass. Likewise for him and so on and so forth; it was a popular game amongst revellers that usually brought out the humorous side in all of the participants.

Isabella felt so deliciously inebriated that she was now spilling more than she was drinking. They both ended up giggling and laughing.

'One last drink for you and then to bed with you, young lady,' he said as he went to the side cabinet and poured it for her.

After she had downed her drink, Robert scooped up a very happy Isabella into his arms and took her to his bedchamber. He quickly turned the knob on the door with a momentarily free hand and elbowed it open, manoeuvring his way into the room and to lay her upon the bed.

'Oh, Robert, I do love you so much,' she slurred in her happy drunken haze.

'And I you, my love,' he replied.

'The room is going around and around and I do feel so dizzy,' she laughed as she put a hand to her spinning head.

As Isabella lay on the bed she suddenly started to feel odd, she was hot and she began to sweat. She could hear Robert's voice but it had become muffled and strange. She felt him stroke her hair and gently kiss her forehead, but she now felt too ill to respond. Although she could hear him, she couldn't quite make out what he was saying to her. More declarations of love she thought still feeling uninclined.

Whilst Isabella lay in muddled confusion, Robert quickly ran down the back stairs to open the back door and beckoned his visitor to follow him quickly. Isabella heard Robert's voice again but this time more clearly.

'Come in, Mrs Gates,' he growled as they arrived at the bedroom door.

Then she heard another voice, 'Ok me dear, you gived her the potion that I gived you earlier this morning, I see.'

Was that the voice of a woman? Isabella thought with foggy confusion. She tried hard to open her eyes but it was as if they were glued shut. She tried to sit up but she couldn't. She began to feel very frightened. She couldn't concentrate and she couldn't make out the words that were being said.

'There that's nice an' drowsy. She won't feel a thing sir, really she won't.'

Robert recalled the stench of stale alcohol and filth that he had smelled on the woman that morning when he first visited her, and she still had the same vile odour. He felt disgust for the woman who had been his second port of call that day, after he had visited the jeweller.

Mrs Gates was a short, rough-looking woman of large proportions. She wore a straw hat that had seen better days and her grey hair was straggling unkempt beneath it. Her face was aged, plump and podgy, and there were hairs growing from her chin. Her clothes were filthy and covered in stains, of what, he could not guess or maybe again he could? It made him physically shudder.

She opened up her bag with her large, rough,

working hands and took out some metal rods together with some rags that looked none-too-clean. When she spoke her voice had a coarse accent. 'Yer can go, sir, if it pleases yer, but it would be betta if yer stays to hold her down should it be necessary,' Mrs Gates said through a rotting toothed smile.

'Yes, I will stay,' Robert snapped.

He had lain Isabella across the width of the bed with her legs dangling down over the edge of one side of it, as instructed by Mrs Gates earlier that day. He positioned himself at the other side of the bed and held her head in his hands, stroking her now very wet hair. She was groaning and moving her head from side to side in a fevered restlessness.

'Ok, dearie, let's have them feet up on the edge of the bed shall we?' Mrs Gates said as she roughly pulled up Isabella skirts and placed her legs up and apart in a frog-like position. Then she crudely pushed back her petticoats to expose the area that required her attention.

'There we go's, sir, if you would be kind enough to hang onto her knees and keep um there for me to do me work, sir.'

Robert obliged with disgust as Mrs Gates turned to her bag again and took out a half-empty bottle of gin and took a large swig.

'Tis thirsty work this, sir,' she said, as she put a

thick grubby finger inside of Isabella, and twisted it around.

Isabella began to stir and said, 'No, Robert, not tonight please, you're hurting me. I don't feel very well.'

The old hag let out a chuckle, 'Oh you'll love it in a minute dearie, that yer will,' she said as she removed her fingers. Robert shot her a look of distaste.

'Now yer holds on to her tight mind, if yer wants the job done proper,' the wizened old woman said as she inserted one of the rods inside of Isabella and guided it with a twisting motion.

Isabella cried out in pain and started to struggle, but she could feel that someone held her legs in a vice-like grip and was unable to get free. The pain was excruciating, stabbing through her belly and right up inside her. In her drugged state, although she was feeling the pain, it was a strange pain, almost as if it was happening to someone else, but pain it was nonetheless.

Mrs Gates stood gazing into the air as if she were deep in thought. She sniffed and wiped her dripping nose with the back of her hand. She pressed down hard on the poor pregnant woman's belly. Isabella, still semi-conscious, let out a piercing scream of pain and was calling for Robert to help her.

'Gates, how long must this go on?' Robert demanded, as he was now feeling so wretched having to hold Isabella down so firmly and having to watch the horrific work of the abortionist. He had no time for this low life of necessary evil.

'All but done, sir,' she said as she removed the rods and wiped the blood off them onto Isabella's stockinged legs by way of cleaning the instruments of her profession. She then grabbed the dirty rags and mopped up between Isabella's legs. 'There we is, sir, now I'll just 'elp you get her into bed and she'll be fine in a couple a days.'

The two of them manoeuvred the half-conscious, bleeding and whimpering Isabella into the bed and under the covers.

Robert regretted bitterly that Isabella had gone and got herself a belly and had had to go through this ghastly experience; she should have taken more care. He turned to the ugly old woman as he thrust the money into her sweaty, grubby, blood-stained hand and shouted at her with loathing,

'Get out, you old hag. Go down the back stairs the way you came in, and be quiet and quick about it.'

'Ok, me dear. Should yer need me again yer knows where's to find me, don't yer?' She chuckled as she took another swig on her bottle and put her instruments and rags back into her bag then disappeared out of the bedchamber clasping her blood money to her person. Robert rushed to the chamber pot thinking he might vomit.

Sarah, hearing the screams and the commotion coming from the master's bedchamber down the one flight of stairs from her own and fearing for Miss Isabella, had crept onto the back staircase to see what was going on and she saw and recognised 'Old Mother Gates', as she was none too affectionately known, as she let herself out by the back door.

Sarah gave a loud gasp and quickly clasped her hand to her mouth, hoping that the master had not heard her. But she was safe from being discovered as Isabella's groaning was so desperate and wretched that no other sound could have been heard.

Sarah went back to bed knowing there was nothing she could do right now. It pained her so, that she couldn't even comfort her poor miss, as the master was still in the room.

Oh that mad man, she thought to herself, *with all those empty promises that he had given to my poor lady. How could he have called in Old Mother Gates?* She felt anger and sadness as she quietly cried herself to sleep.

Robert, not wanting Isabella to know that he had

done away with the baby and wanting her to believe that she had lost the child in the natural way, dared not leave the room and give the game away. He was worried that her noises would be heard by Sarah. But could not bear the thought of lying next to Isabella in her state, so instead positioned himself in the large armchair by the window and had to endure the continual sounds of Isabella's groans and whimpers of pain throughout the night.

* * *

Next morning, Sarah, having had a restless night, got up earlier than usual and went downstairs to clear away the previous night's plates and dishes and contemplate what she could do to help Isabella.

She prepared Robert's breakfast, wishing that she could poison him for what he had done to her miss.

Robert came into the breakfast room and helped himself to something to eat, 'Sarah,' he said, 'your mistress is not feeling well this morning, too much to drink last night, I wager. You may have heard her drunken moans. So leave her be until she is ready to raise herself.'

'Yes, sir,' said Sarah as normally as she could.

As soon as Robert left the house Sarah instructed

Bruce to clear away the dishes from the morning meal and start the daily chores while she went to help Miss Isabella. She knocked on the bedchamber door and when she heard no answer, let herself in and was aghast at the sight that confronted her. Isabella was lying quite still, with beads of sweat on her forehead, her hair was wringing wet and she was softly groaning in pain and delirium.

'Miss Isabella,' Sarah spoke quietly. Isabella did not respond, 'Miss Isabella.' Sarah tried again a little louder. Again no response. Sarah, knowing Mrs Gates' trade, gently eased back the bed covers and gasped at the horror that met her eyes. The bed sheet that Isabella was lying on was soaked with sticky dark blood and she was still dressed in her lovely yellow-and-blue gown of the night before, which was now heavily stained with blood.

'Oh, my God,' Sarah said aloud and wondered for a moment what on earth she could do. Her answer came to her almost in an instant. Although, due to her scarred face, she didn't often venture out, she knew that to help Isabella she had no choice.

She ran to her room and found the large-brimmed hat she used to help cover her face and the pair of lace gloves to hide her hands. She found the embroidered handkerchief Isabella had given her to hold to her nose and also help her hide her scarred features. She ran down the main staircase that was normally forbidden to her, but it was the quickest route. She quickly told Bruce what had happened, in chosen words for a young boy to understand.

'That bastard devil, I will do for him, I will, Sarah, I will,' he angrily said.

'Bruce, I feel the same as you but we must not show our feelings or we could be thrown out of here and how then could we help our miss? Do not mention this to a living soul.'

'I will do anything, Sarah. Fear not, you can trust me, really you can. I will do whatever you tell me for Miss Isabella,' Bruce said, as he put his hand to his head with disbelief, mixed with concern.

'I do not expect the master back yet, but should he arrive, tell him that I have had to go to the market,' she said.

'Oh no, Sarah. He knows you don't go out much.'

'Oh, Bruce. Then make something up. Anything. But I don't expect him back yet anyway, little one.'

Sarah then went out into the streets in search of Mrs Barbara Newman. She had not as yet made the acquaintance of Mrs Newman but she knew that if anyone could help, she could.

As she searched the streets, she looked up at the

washed-out wooden shop signs that creaked as they swung back and forth, portraying the businesses that were being carried out therein. She hurried along the grimy cobbled streets, holding her handkerchief firmly over her face, as much to help block out the London stench as to hide her blemishes.

First, she tried the drapers shop and enquired whether Mrs Newman had been in shopping that morning. She remembered that when Miss Isabella told her of her daily events she spoke of the shops and places that she and Barbara had visited. The apothecary and the dressmaker's were next on her list.

The proprietors of these businesses were none too happy to see a lone member of the serving classes, whom they did not recognise, stepping foot into their establishments, making enquiries about their valued customer, the wealthy Mrs Newman, so they quickly ushered her out with a few cruel words to go along with their unpleasant manner.

Although Sarah felt the shame of this abuse, she kept on going for the sake of her miss. The poor housemaid was getting so desperate to find Barbara that she almost couldn't breathe from the panic of it all, but then when Sarah entered the Coffee House her search finally came to an end, for when she enquired if anyone had seen Mrs Newman as she had an urgent message for her, Barbara herself heard the girl and had a feeling that this was the Sarah, Isabella had described.

'I am Barbara Newman. Are you Sarah?' she said kindly.

'Oh thank goodness I've found you,' Sarah said as she burst into tears of relief. Barbara sat the girl down and waited patiently while she relayed her story of the screams that she heard, and of Old Mother Gates presence and the blood she had found her poor delirious lady lying in. She told of how she knew that her mistress loved her baby and would not have had this abortion willingly, and how Robert must have got her very drunk to knock her out somehow. She told of what the master had said that morning about leaving the mistress alone until she was ready to rise by herself.

'Thank you, Sarah,' Barbara said calmly. 'Now do not worry. I will get some help for your mistress. Your master is out, I take it?'

Sarah nodded, 'Yes, he should be gone for most of the day.' She wiped her eyes with her handkerchief.

Barbara instructed Sarah as to what she must do to help her mistress and then said, 'Now go to Miss Isabella and I will be there soonest. I will enter by the servants' door as I do not want to be announced to any prying eyes.'

'Thank you, Mrs Barbara,' Sarah said with a

curtsy and rushed off into the streets again.

She ran back to the house and entered via the mews at the back of the building through the hallway and up the main stairs. It was only when she arrived on the top step of the first floor did she realise that someone was in the bedchamber talking but it didn't sound like the mistress' voice.

As her nerves got the better of her, she prayed it was not the master, then with a rush of strength her bravery returned, she quickly turned the knob to the bedchamber and rushed in. She gasped with shock as she saw the figure sitting on the side of the bed, for in her fear, for a very few moments she did not recognise the frame of Bruce the houseboy.

'Oh thank goodness, Bruce it's only you,' she said with a sigh of relief, 'now go downstairs and bring me some water for Miss Isabella to drink. The clean stuff mind!'

Sarah wrung out a cloth with the water in the jug on the wash stand and placed it onto Isabella's forehead. 'Oh. Mrs Barbara do hurry,' she said aloud.

Isabella, began to stir and opened her eyes. 'Sarah' she said, her voice very weak.

'Yes, miss, I'm here.'

'What has happened to me, Sarah?' a distressed Isabella managed to ask.

'I'm so sorry, Miss Isabella,' Sarah hesitated, 'but it seems that you have lost your baby.'

Barbara had told Sarah not to let Isabella know that what had happened was Robert's doing as this would distress her too much and she needed all her strength if she was to recover from this appalling business.

Isabella cried out in a very weak voice, 'No, no, not my baby! My baby, my baby.' She began to sob and moan uncontrollably. Just then Bruce entered the bedchamber accompanied by Barbara and a man carrying a bag.

'I have brought Dr Fairfax, my physician, to help your mistress,' Barbara addressed Sarah as she looked over to the bed and her eyes fell upon her dear friend who looked almost unrecognisable. Barbara was shocked. 'Damn the man, the devil take him straight to hell,' she cursed under her breath, but quickly regained her composure and directed words to Sarah again, 'You go about your duties, Sarah,' she ordered the anxious servant, 'I will call you when there is anything for you to know.'

Dr Fairfax approached the bed, drew back the sheets and even he was sickened at the sight that met his eyes, but this was not the first time that he had seen the handiwork of Old Mother Gates. He quickly removed his coat and as gently as he could he began to examine Isabella. She weakly uttered indistinct almost inaudible sounds of pain as she was just about conscious again. Barbara at her side was holding her hand and tried to sooth her as much as she could. The doctor took a large inhalation of breath and as he slowly exhaled he shook his head and shot Barbara a look that said that there was little to no hope.

'Doctor, I insist that you try something, anything,' Barbara commanded in a loud voice. 'Do something. Anything is better than nothing. Please, Doctor,' she urged.

Doctor Fairfax walked to the window and stared down into the street below, deep in thought. Barbara looked on. She had known the doctor for a long time and knew that he would do his best. After a few minutes of quiet deliberation, he turned, looked at the concern on Barbara face and said, 'Very well. Let's get some clearing done here. For a start I need some clean sheets and lots of water that has been boiled and cooled. I've seen this procedure done before but I'm not sure what part of it made the difference so we will try it all,' he said. He returned to the bedside and opened his medical bag. Barbara called Sarah to come and help and bring what was necessary.

'What time do we have before Bloom gets home?'

Barbara asked a very worried Sarah.

'We should have about four hours. I've told Bruce to keep an eye out for him.'

'Well done, Sarah,' Barbara commended.

Isabella, recognising Sarah's voice gave out a painful groan, 'Help me. Help me, Sarah,' she managed to murmur.

'She knows you're here, Sarah. Now get her to take this,' Dr Fairfax said, as he handed some laudanum to the girl.

Once the laudanum had started to work they all set about trying to save Isabella's life. They removed the blood-soaked clothes and sheets as quickly and gently as they could and held onto her hands which were reaching out for theirs. She gripped them as hard as she could with the little strength that she had left.

As Isabella finally succumbed totally to the laudanum, the doctor was able to start the procedure and as he had surmised the remnants of the pregnancy still remained.

Sarah wiped the patient's brow with a cool damp cloth, whilst the doctor set about his work. Sarah couldn't bear the sound of the muffled whimpers of pain that told her that her lady could still feel through the sleeping draught.

'Be strong, Miss Isabella, be strong,' she

whispered, just in case Isabella could hear her.

Dr Fairfax worked on until finally, he said, 'That's it now, that's all I can do. I have at last managed to stem the bleeding. The next steps are up to Isabella, you Sarah and the Almighty. But if she survives I think it goes without saying that her ever having a child again is virtually impossible.'

While the doctor washed the blood from his hands in the bowl provided, he instructed Sarah how to best look after her patient.

'Sarah, I'm leaving you in charge. Make sure she drinks plenty of clean water.' He then handed her a bottle of the laudanum and a small bottle of herbal mixture. 'Make sure she takes these. One for pain and help her to sleep, the other to make her well. She must take these, Sarah,' the doctor emphasised.

'Yes, Doctor,' she said.

Then Barbara and Sarah, having enlisted the help of Bruce, changed the sheets again.

'Now, you keep your eyes to yourself Bruce Wilson,' Sarah ordered.

'I wouldn't look, Sarah, really I wouldn't,' he said, as he had already averted his tear-filled eyes.

They somehow managed to get Isabella into a fresh clean nightgown. Then the four of them, each taking hold of a section of the sheet that was beneath the now unconscious Isabella and carrying with both hands, edged their way as gently as they could along the corridor into Isabella's own bedchamber for her to recover.

'If she makes it through the night we have a fighting chance,' the doctor said, as they helped Sarah gently lay the clean covers over their patient's listless body and made her as comfortable as they were able.

'Now no word of this to the master, do you hear me?' said Barbara. 'You will have to say that she is unwell, she has some sort of ague or other. She is in her room recovering. Do I make myself clear on this to all of you, he must not suspect that you know anything of the baby or of our being here today. Do you understand?'

They all knew exactly what Barbara was telling them.

'You must get word to me at the coffee house and let me know how Isabella is faring. I know you can put a few written sentences together, Sarah, so either come in person or send word, and don't worry, I will ensure that the treatment that you experienced on the streets today will never happen to you again or to young Bruce here,' Barbara instructed.

'Yes, I will, Mrs Barbara and thank you so much for helping our lady,' Sarah said as she curtsied.

Barbara turned and looked once more at her precious friend lying so still in the fresh bed.

'Lord have mercy,' she said and those present repeated the same words after her.

The doctor and Barbara let themselves out through the servants' entrance, through the mews and hurried along the streets.

'Quick, Bruce we must ready the master's dinner. I will be going to check on the mistress whenever I can but I will need your help to save me from detection, Can you do that?'

'Of course I can, Sarah. I won't let anything happen to you or Miss Isabella. I will sleep in the kitchen tonight, in case you need me.'

'Thank you, Bruce darling. But first you must quickly run and tell your mother that you are staying here tonight to save her worrying. Now let's hurry!'

* * *

Robert was in no rush to get back home. He knew that when he had left the house that morning, Isabella was not in a good way. Having spent the night in the chair he was tired.

This whole experience with Mrs Gates was something that a man of my standing should not have to be put through. This was women's work. Mrs Gates had said that all would be well in a couple of days, so she must be a little better today and fully recovered by *tomorrow or at the latest by the next evening, I wonder how long it would be before I recover from the ordeal of all this,* he thought selfishly.

He trusted that she had managed to clean herself up and sort out the mess that she had made on the bed. He hoped that she had been able to get rid of the blood-stained bedding without any of the servants knowing and he expected that they had got something good to eat for his dinner.

He walked into the house and was met by Sarah coming up the kitchen stairs.

'Good evening, sir,' Sarah steeled herself to say, 'Bruce is on his way upstairs with your hot water, sir.' Remembering what Barbara had told her to say, Sarah continued, 'Miss Isabella is not well, sir, she has some ague or another and she is resting in her room. She is sleeping now as she is very tired. I will be serving dinner in an hour if it pleases you, sir.'

'Yes, of course, Sarah. I will be down in time.'

Robert went to his bedchamber. He was glad that Isabella was not there and was sleeping. He didn't want to see her at the moment. He needed time to get over the events of last evening. He washed in the large bowl and dressed for dinner having his usual brandy as he readied himself. He heard the gong and descended the stairs, walked into the dining room and helped himself to the dishes set before him.

As Robert ate, Sarah crept up the back stairs with some soup and bread to try to tempt Isabella into eating something. She entered the bedchamber.

'Miss Isabella,' she called gently. 'I have some warm broth for you, if you feel that you can manage it. Here, let me help you sit up.'

Isabella, not quite awake, opened her eyes slowly and was barely able to whisper the words through the pain.

'I'm sorry, Sarah, I can't sit up or eat anything.'

'Very well, miss, but you must take this. The doctor left it for you, it will help you with the pain and help you to sleep,' Sarah said as she poured some laudanum and the mixture onto a spoon and let Isabella sip from it.

The doctor? Isabella thought. She was not quite sure of the events that had taken place that day but she didn't have the strength and was in too much pain to question any of Sarah's words and obediently did as she was being told.

Sarah touched Isabella's forehead and was relieved to find that her mistress's fever had dropped slightly.

'Is Robert home?' Isabella managed to whisper.

'Yes, miss. But Mrs Barbara said that the master wouldn't want us to know about the baby, so we were to let him think that we understood you to have the ague and that you would be well again soon. Mrs Barbara also said that we were not to tell the master of her or the doctor's presence here earlier today. Do you know what I'm telling you, Miss Isabella? You must understand,' Sarah urged.

Vague memories of what had happened were running in and out of Isabella's mind but some flashbacks were too painful to retain.

'Yes, I understand very well and thank you, Sarah for what you did for me today.'

Isabella didn't hear Sarah's reply of, 'I'm so sorry about your baby,' as she had mercifully fallen into a deep sleep.

* * *

Robert, having finished his meal, left the house in search of some of his fellow gamblers and friends for a night's merriment.

He went to Barbara Newman's gaming house. Barbara looked up as Robert entered the halls accompanied by his cohort, Henry Brookes. The rooms were well lit with plenty of candelabras and oil lamps to illuminate the proceedings at the tables. This was necessary to stop any double-dealing or sleight of hand that a trickster may use to cheat the house of any of its profits. "Floorwalkers" were employed to keep an eye on any questionable activity and to maintain a presence of security in the rooms that were fast becoming thick with gentlemen's cigar smoke. The rooms were busy this evening with well-dressed gentlemen and ladies in their finery.

Barbara was so incensed, she had to stop the urge of walking right over to Robert and land a punch full on his chin, as she thought *I wish I could knee him in the nutmegs. If I were a man, I would challenge him to a duel and be done with the bastard scoundrel once and for all. How dare he cross my threshold with my poor Isabella fighting for her life?*

But she knew that she had to maintain her self-control for Isabella's sake. Barbara knew that Robert wouldn't think twice about turning the poor, desperate innocent onto the streets at any sign of a threat or nuisance to him. Then have the nerve to go after Thomas for the balance of his loan. He was a blackguard of the worst order and he was to be treated with the utmost caution.

She made her way to where the two men were standing.

'Good evening, gentleman,' Barbara gushed with a smile to help cover her repulsion. 'How may we be of service to you this evening? A glass of our finest wine or brandy perhaps? You might like to try the cards, or is it to be a game of dice? The tables are looking good tonight. We have many players here this evening.' The men gave their order for drinks and Barbara signalled to the serving girls to bring them over. The men moved around the tables looking for what might take their fancy.

The evening progressed but Lady Luck was not walking with Robert tonight so he moved into the salon, where players could lounge around discussing business or just take a rest from the tables and chat. It was not as brightly lit as the gaming room, which made it more comfortable with plush red velvet sofas for the lounging. There were two writing desks set against the far wall with paper and writing requirements for the use of note making or more often than not for a client to write a promissory note of intention to pay or to sign over some valuables to settle his debt. This facility was usually for the regulars and only at the proprietor's discretion. Scattered around the room were tables, upon which were placed boxes of cigars for the customer's indulgence and added to their bill.

The serving girls, who were all very pretty, but were not for the touching, under Barbara's strict house rules, brought copious amounts of liquor for the partaking, in this more relaxed part of the gaming house.

Due to his state of mind, following the events of the previous night, Robert got himself mercilessly drunk and it was left to his friends, who were also a little worse for drink, to settle his account with Barbara and somehow manage to make sure he arrived back at Berkeley Street in one piece.

They pushed him in through his front door and pulled it closed shut behind him. He managed to stagger into the library and he curled himself up into one of the chairs and immediately fell into a drunken sleep.

* * *

As morning came Sarah, having first checked on Miss Isabella, went down the back stairs to the kitchen and found Bruce sitting at the table.

'The master's not in his bedchamber,' he said.

'Well I know he wasn't with Miss Isabella,' Sarah said. 'I assume he has stayed out again with some of his friends.' This was a regular occurrence and no cause for concern. The two went about their daily duties.

Sarah went into the library and a vile stench met her nose, she had found Robert. He was asleep, stinking of booze and in a state of much disarray; the normally dignified dandy had wet his breeches and had vomited on the floor.

What a mess to clear up, Sarah thought with loathing, *but at least he hasn't been able to climb the stairs and pester Miss Isabella in his drunkenness.*

'What a mercy,' she said aloud.

At that point Bruce came into the room and when he saw the scene in front of his eyes he exclaimed, 'Well, will someone shake me. The Peacock's only gone and pissed himself.'

This set Sarah off into a fit of laughter that she had to stifle with her hand, 'Oh. Bruce, you are so funny, but hush darling, don't let his nibs hear or we will be in real trouble.'

He looked at her with a coy smile and said, 'What me, Sarah?' which made Sarah have to hold back another laugh.

Then, together, they roused the master, very gently for fear of his drink induced temper. Bruce helped Robert, still belching and farting, up the stairs to his bedchamber, where he fell on the bed with an extra hard push from Bruce for good measure. *That's for my miss*, he thought to himself. Bruce had no intention of helping the master to get cleaned up and out of his soiled clothes. Today he knew that his lack of duty would go undetected.

Sometime later, when Robert had slept off some of the drink and he was able to stand unaided, he managed to get himself cleaned up and changed. He felt so ill that he didn't even have the strength to shout for the house boy to bring him some clean water, so instead he found some cloth to wipe himself down. He felt the full benefit of a hangover, which he showed remarkably well in his demeanour. He got himself down the stairs and entered the morning room.

Sarah had baked some bread and made coffee for when the master was ready. He drank down the coffee and threw the bread across the room with much contempt. Then he made his way out of the door, he felt he had to try to conduct some kind of business today. Sarah had heard earlier from Jack that the recent silk shipment was still in the lighters and the men were trying to get it ashore and this would take up a lot of the day.

Poor Jack, he'll be for it today, she thought, as she made her way to her mistress' room.

She found that Isabella, although still slightly

under the spell of the laudanum she had administered to her over the course of the night, had started to come round. The ghostly pallor was slowly leaving her cheeks and she seemed a little brighter. *Dare I think that the doctor, with the blessing of the Almighty, has saved her life?* She prayed so.

'Hello, Miss Isabella. How are you feeling today?' Sarah asked softly.

'Oh, Sarah. I am in much pain. I've never known the like before. Is this due to the...' she could barely bring the words to form in her mouth 'the miscarriage'? The words caught in her throat and turned into sobs.

'Partly, yes, miss, I believe so. But you had some um... complications and Mrs Barbara had to bring the doctor to help. The master knows nothing of this, do you remember what I said to you yesterday?' said Sarah.

Isabella had to concentrate hard to remember, her head was still woozy from the tincture of opium.

'Yes, I remember. Was that only yesterday? Oh, my poor, poor, baby.'

'Yes, miss, I know.' Sarah soothed. 'But you look so much better today and the bleeding has almost stopped now. I can't believe it. We all feared for your life yesterday. But I think the doctor has done a good job. Thank goodness. Now I want you to really try to have some of this broth today. It is what my mother gave to me, God rest her soul, and I swear it's what helped me recover from the smallpox.'

'I will try, Sarah. Thank you,' Isabella managed to sip quite a lot of the cooled broth from Sarah's small dish, but the effort tired her very quickly. Sarah laid her back against the pillows.

'Now here, just take a little more of this laudanum and the mixture, Miss Isabella, so that you can sleep the pain away and I will get word to Mrs Barbara that you have improved a little.'

'Thank you, Sarah,' her grateful mistress said as she once again drifted into that welcome place of oblivion.

* * *

The next days that followed were much the same, with the exception that with each new day, Isabella seemed to be getting a little better, albeit still very distraught about the child that she had lost. She was now able to sit up quite easily and Sarah was able to get her to take more food and drink. Bruce was ordered to bring in a bowl of warm water so that Sarah could give her lady a refreshing wash.

Bruce approached Isabella and spoke to her for

the first time since she had been confined to bed.

'Miss Isabella, I am so glad to see that you are looking so much better. It makes me ache, it does really, to see you hurting so. Get well soon, my lady,' he said and, as if embarrassed by his outpouring of emotion, turned and hurried out of the room. Isabella was really quite touched by this outburst, from the normally shy young lad.

Sarah set about washing her mistress and she gently brushed her hair and tied it back with a bow.

* * *

Every day Isabella asked after Robert, even though Sarah had told her that he had said that it would be better for him to see Isabella once she was up and about again and fully recovered from whatever illness had befallen her.

In truth, Robert had been spending more and more time away from the house. Sometimes he would stay with Henry Brookes or at other friend's houses, sometimes at the club and sometimes goodness knows where. He could be gone for days on end. Sarah knew this should not be disclosed to her miss as it would not aide her recovery.

Isabella lay in her bed. The physical pain had

eased quite considerably and she was almost back to her old self again. She had arranged for Sarah to secrete a book from the library for her to read. It had been just over six weeks now since she had lost the baby and Robert had not been to see her in all that time. She wondered if he was cross with her in some way. With Robert's absence and the loss of her baby her misery knew no bounds. She still wanted to sleep a lot as the mental pain was almost worse than the physical one.

Then one morning there was a knock on her door and Isabella just managed to hide the book under the bed covers before Robert entered the room and was standing there in front of her.

'Oh. Robert. I have missed you so much, where have you been?' she cried.

'I missed you too, of course. But I have been busy and I thought it better for you to recover,' he said as he sat down on the bed beside her.

Good gracious, you do look pale and ill. Not at all like my Isabella. It's a good job that I kept my distance. I hope that it is not something that I can catch, he thought to himself.

Isabella steeled herself to say the next words, 'Robert, I have some bad news to tell you. We have lost our beautiful baby. I am afraid that I have miscarried and now it is no more. Oh, Robert I am so sorry.'

Robert took her hands in his, he genuinely felt some sadness knowing Isabella was suffering so.

'Well, I had guessed that was the case, my sweet. But it is best for you to get yourself better now and not let any other worry enter your head.'

Isabella cried in Robert's arms as he stroked her hair. *Robert, I do so wonder if you still want to marry me*, she thought as she remembered Robert's words which now echoed through her mind, "Of course I will marry you, if you bear my child," he had said. *But I am not carrying your child now, am I?* She worried.

'My love, I need to tell you that I am going away on urgent business for the next couple of weeks and Sarah will be here to look after you. Benson will be, as always, looking after the business side of things and should you need Jack for anything send the boy to him,' Robert said.

'No, Robert, no. I just can't bear being without you again. It has been just awful you being apart from me all this time,' Isabella protested.

'Well, look here. I'm going away on business and I will be back in a couple of weeks. This will give you a good chance to get fully recovered. Then we can start our life again. You just get well, my darling,' he said to soften his first words.

Isabella could see the wisdom of his words. She

knew that she was sleeping more than she was awake and although she was saddened to her very soul, she accepted that Robert had business to carry out. She also knew that she had little choice in the matter.

CHAPTER 6

Next day, whilst Sarah was tidying the master's study, she found a letter of invitation lying idle on his desk. She was just able to read the words upon it. It seemed the business trip that Bloom was so keen to attend had something to do with this invitation.

It read, "Lord Wokingham requests the pleasure of Mr Robert Bloom. . . ." Sarah read the further words that she could understand "Formally invited for the duration of the season", *so he was to stay with a wealthy landowner friend, was he? While Miss Isabella lay in her bed recovering from the atrocity she is suffering due to his hand.* She took note of the date and address. He was to travel to Berkshire the very next day. She sent a message informing Barbara of these facts.

Barbara, thus far, had felt that it would be rather foolhardy to visit her friend for fear of Robert returning home at an unannounced hour. But she had kept in constant contact with Sarah with notes being delivered and collected by Bruce. He, being a popular lad, could get around town quite quickly, he knew many a trader and the like, who travelled by horse and cart and it was no trouble for him to hitch a ride to get to his destination swiftly. Even the drivers of the larger coaches would often slow down when they saw him, so that he could hop on the back. This enabled any correspondence to go back and forth between Sarah and Barbara without too much of a delay.

Sarah was then pleased that Robert was going away as his absence would permit her miss to receive much welcome visitors.

Barbara's reply told Sarah that she would be bringing Dr Fairfax with her the day after to visit Isabella. She also informed her that it was now common knowledge that Bloom would be going to the country for the season, for he had been bragging about it in her gaming house the night before and he could be gone for some time, but on no account was she to let her mistress know the duration of time he may be absent as this would cause her distress.

Although Sarah did not like to deceive her mistress, she trusted that Mrs Barbara knew what was best.

The master being away would allow her lady time to heal and not be subjected to any unwanted physical advances. Sarah knew a period of convalescence was what was needed if Isabella was to be well again, even at the cost of her mistress' distress at being without her master.

* * *

The next morning Robert bade his farewell to Isabella, after giving Sarah and Bruce his final instructions for the house to run smoothly in his absence.

'Sarah, I'm sure the housekeeper will be up and about soon and she will carry on in my stead,' Robert said. Sarah, with head held low, bobbed her usual curtsy in reply.

The housekeeper, he said. The Housekeeper! He doesn't call her that. She repeated these words in her head. *Oh my poor miss. He surely is a mad man.*

Bruce, who had shot a look of shock at Sarah upon hearing these words, cursed the man under his breath. He had happily helped pack the master's clothes into the trunks early that morning and had given the coachman a hand to get the luggage aloft. Robert boarded the carriage he had hired for himself for the purpose of the journey and set off to Berkshire.

As soon as Robert's coach was out of sight, Sarah went to see Isabella and tried to comfort her mistress in her distress.

'Sarah, I don't remember an awful lot about that night, you know when I was poorly,' her words trailed off, unable to be spoken. 'But, I do remember hearing a female voice in the room with Robert and I. Was it you, Sarah?'

'No. miss, not I. I think you were a little um… delirious at the time. There was no other lady here, as I am aware,' she said. Sarah knew that she had not lied to her mistress as Old Mother Gates would never be considered a lady.

'Robert gave me a wonderful brooch that night. Do you know where it is?' Isabella asked.

'Yes, miss, I placed it here in the drawer for you.' In truth Sarah couldn't bear the sight of it for she felt sure as to why it had been given to Isabella.

A brooch in exchange for a baby. Sarah shuddered when she thought of it. She hadn't told her mistress that the doctor had said that she would never be able to bear a child again as she felt it was a subject better suited to Barbara or the doctor himself, but her very knowledge of it was burning a hole in her heart.

* * *

The next day Barbara arrived as had been arranged, along with her was Dr Fairfax. They entered as before through the servants' entrance.

'My darling,' Barbara said and with a rustle of skirts she rushed over to Isabella's side and very gently gave her a hug.

'Oh, Barbara, I have missed you so. I have had the most awful of times,' Isabella said, finding comfort in Barbara's very presence.

Isabella was dressed in a white night gown and had progressed from lying almost flat and still to a raised sitting position supported by several pillows, which were in crisp white with frilled edges. Sarah had brushed Isabella's hair and had tied it up with a blue ribbon; she had also applied a little colour to her lips and cheeks to make her look and feel more presentable.

Barbara was so pleased to see that Isabella had improved greatly from the last time that she had seen her. She had brought Isabella a gift of a French perfume bottle in Isabella's favourite colours of blue and white, with a pretty delicate design.

'It is exquisite thank you so much,' Isabella said, genuinely taken with the beautiful gift.

Dr Fairfax moved forward and said, 'Shall we get the examination over and then I can leave you ladies to your tea and chatting.'

Sarah excused herself and left the room to allow Isabella a little more privacy while Barbara held the patient's hand as the doctor started his examination. When it was over he replaced the covers and sat on the side of the bed and spoke kindly to Isabella.

'I am so glad to say that you are well over the worst and that everything has healed nicely, mostly due I'm sure to a very good nurse who has been looking after you so diligently. It is nothing short of a miracle, I would say.'

Barbara gave Isabella's hand a long squeeze.

'I'm so happy that you are so well, my darling,' she said as she turned to look over to Dr Fairfax, 'and thank you, Doctor, as I'm sure without your work we would surely have lost my dear friend.'

The doctor smiled and continued, 'Has anyone told you yet, my dear, of the unfortunate consequence of this... um... miscarriage that you have had?' The doctor had been briefed by Barbara that he must not let Isabella know that she had in fact suffered an abortion at the instigation of Robert.

'What do you mean?' Isabella looked puzzled.

'Well, my dear,' continued the kindly doctor, 'because your miscarriage had some complications, I am afraid you will be unable to carry any more children. I am truly sorry, that I bring you these sad tidings, my dear.' Isabella gave a gasp and a look of horror crossed her face.

'No, Dr Fairfax. You must be wrong. I must have children I really must,' she sobbed.

'I'm so sorry, my dear,' he said as he patted her hand with such sympathy it made Isabella cry even more. The doctor got up from the bed and said, 'Well you just get well now. I will take my leave of you ladies and on my way out, I will instruct Sarah regarding the next stages of your recovery, which should allow you time out of bed and moving around a little more and I will also ask her to bring you up some tea. Goodbye, my dear. Goodbye, Mrs Newman.'

The ladies both thanked him and bade him farewell as he left the bedchamber and went down the stairs in search of Sarah.

Barbara, try as she might, found there was no comforting the distraught Isabella. *Damn that bastard, Bloom* she thought, *he has robbed Isabella of ever being a mother and having a child of her own*. Barbara was also aware that Robert had been visiting Mary these past weeks, obviously, as Isabella was not for his pleasure at this present time. But this news was not for Isabella's ears.

Isabella was tearful all of that day and most of the next. When she wasn't crying she was staring into space, almost a lifeless figure not wanting anything or anyone. She could not believe the cruel twist of fate that life had bestowed upon her.

'Oh, Sarah! Never to have Robert's child ever, it is too much for me to bear. Oh, how I wish that he were here by my side and not in some far-off town. Do you think that he will still love me when he finds out about this news? Do you think that he will still marry me?' she asked through her tears.

Sarah did all she could to help comfort her but it wasn't until Monday morning that Isabella finally stopped crying and began to accept in her mind the awful blow that was facing her. Thinking things over, she had come to a decision. She asked for Sarah and Bruce to come to her bedchamber as she wanted to speak with them on a matter of some urgency.

Sarah and Bruce stood quietly by the side of the bed, both realising that this conversation was that of a serious one and not to be taken informally.

Isabella spoke with an unusual voice of authority.

'Firstly, I would like to thank you both so very much for your kindness and attention that you have afforded me over these past few weeks. Without which I am aware that I should surely have perished.'

'You are very welcome, miss…' Sarah, began but Isabella raised her hand to stop any other from talking and for her to carry on speaking in a tone of great solemnity. 'What I am about to say is of the utmost importance to me and I trust that you will never make me repeat it. I am sure you know how I truly value your friendship and the help that you have given to me. I'm sure that you also know that I will not be able to have any more children. Of this, I am greatly troubled. I do not want this ever to be spoken of again in this house or outside of it and certainly Master Robert is not to hear of it at any cost. I have decided it is better for the master not to be bothered with any of this news and must believe all is well with me. You must do this for me. I will not deviate on this. Do you understand me?'

Both Sarah and Bruce nodded and solemnly agreed and gave their oath. They both fell silent as they realised how important this was to their miss and she needed to know that they would obey this order.

Isabella sank back down into the pillows and turned her head away from them with tears running down her face.

My poor miss. You still believe if that devil thinks you are able to have a child that he will marry you, Sarah thought sadly.

Sarah turned to Bruce, 'You run and get some water on to heat so that Miss Isabella can have a nice bath as the doctor ordered.' As she smoothed down the bed covers she gently spoke to Isabella. 'After your bath miss, you can have a little time in the chair by the window and then I will fetch a hot chocolate drink for you,' Sarah said as she then ushered Bruce out of the door.

CHAPTER 7

Clayton House, Berkshire

Robert finally arrived in Berkshire, having had a most uncomfortable and disagreeable journey lasting several hours, with far too many stops for his liking. He alighted from the coach outside the main gates of the estate and the lodge keeper sent word to the coach house that another visitor had arrived.

Two of Wokingham's liveried men arrived with a carriage to transport him through the estate to the grand house that was to be his residence for the next few weeks. Robert, with crumpled attire and covered in dust, was not in good spirits and gruffly ordered his Lordship's coachman to quickly have his trunks transferred to the awaiting conveyance as he climbed aboard. Robert had indicated to the coachman the gifts that he had brought with him, which he ordered were to be handed to his Lordship on arrival at the house. These gifts consisted of a cask of cognac, some boxes of cigars and a wooden caddy full of tea. Although an easy gift for an importer to supply, Robert knew the offerings would be acceptable.

The carriage travelled along the drive, which had a small incline, then, just over the brow of the hill, the magnificent house, although in the distance could be seen in full view. It was of imposing proportions and well-appointed, with lime trees flanking each side of the road standing as if guardians to the fields and woods beyond. On seeing this, his mood lightened quite considerably.

Robert felt exceedingly pleased with himself for having acquired such a fine connection with a member of the aristocracy of such standing. *It is amazing,* he thought to himself, *who one rubs shoulder's with, down at Barbara Newman's gaming rooms.*

* * *

In actual fact, Edward MacGarrett, Lord Edward Wokingham, Earl of Dunclochlan, all heralding the same person, chose to use whichever title suited the occasion to its best advantage and always had an eye for opportunities and potential business. He was at this time in need of an associate with export and import shipping expertise in London. Word had it that Bloom was probably the right man for the job. His Lordship had been watching him at Barbara Newman's on a few occasions to try to get the measure of him. Then, when he was ready, he moved around the tables and had engaged Robert in conversation about Lady Luck, who had been smiling on them both that particular night. This first meeting had taken place a considerably short time ago, but the two men found that they had rather a good rapport with each other and their relationship developed fast.

In fact, Robert had made sure of that, as he had heard tell of this man's wealth. For some time he had known about Lord Wokingham's famous shooting parties, but had not been able to make his acquaintance, now it was all happening at once and Robert could not believe his good fortune when a note requesting his presence was handed to him. He felt rather smug with himself for securing such a coveted invitation to attend one of these grand affairs in Berkshire.

The carriage pulled up at the front steps of the house and, as Robert stepped down, the huge front door was opened wide by a butler in a rather fine livery uniform. Robert could see that Lord Wokingham himself was standing there in the large entrance hall ready to greet him. He quickly mounted the wide stone steps, two at a time and entered the house.

'Robert, my dear fellow, it's very good to see you

again. I hope your trip here has not been too tiring?' Wokingham said as he walked towards him with his hand outstretched in greeting. Robert grasped and shook his hand firmly in a warm gesture.

'Yes, thank you, my lord, but I'm glad the journey is over.'

'Please, my boy. I've told you, do call me Edward.' The two men walked into the ornately decorated long hall. Robert looked around and took in the opulence of the house around him. An enormous chandelier set in the centre of the high ceiling showed off the splendour of the hall with its grand staircase, which had brass inset mahogany hand rails, one on each side. Around the walls he could see portraits of, Robert assumed, the family ancestors. There was a magnificent painting of a white horse with dogs yapping at its heels, in a green field setting. A Stubbs maybe? Robert thought.

From the ground floor, looking up the stairs to the first landing, there on the back wall was a very fine painting; it was so huge that it covered most of the wall itself and took pride of place. It was of his Lordship and whom Robert assumed to be the Countess with their four daughters all wearing a long swathe of the Scottish tartan cloth that belonged to clan MacGarrett, Wokingham being the clan chieftain.

Edward accompanied Robert into a small anteroom where there was a tray holding a pitcher filled with lemon cordial and he was rather grateful for this refreshing drink after his long and dusty ride. He was informed that his luggage was in his rooms and a warm bath was being drawn for him. The thought of a relaxing bath for his tired body and removing the dust from his person after his long journey was most pleasing.

'Robert, please follow my butler, who will direct you to the suite of rooms that have been prepared for you for the duration of your stay. Once you are ready, please make your way down to the Red Library for pre-dinner drinks,' Wokingham said as he indicated the room in question, 'Then, I will be able to present you to my wife, Lady Louisa, and I will introduce you to the rest of the guests.'

'Thank you, Edward, I very much look forward to meeting your wife, her Ladyship,' Robert said.

Although Robert was considered to be comfortably well off, he seldom had the opportunity to keep such company with nobility who had this kind of money and he felt a little out of his depth. He followed the butler to his accommodation. The rooms were luxurious and comfortable. In his sitting room he found a decanter of sherry to which he helped himself. He then bathed and readied himself, looking forward to the night ahead. He felt rather privileged that he had been invited along to this sporting occasion held on such a grand estate. But being no fool, he had the distinct feeling there was more to this invitation than first appeared and he was eager to find out more, but he knew that he would have to wait for Wokingham to make his play.

* * *

Once rested and ready for the evening, dressed in some of his best finery, assisted by a valet, Robert opened the door to his room and found a footman waiting to escort him to the Red Library.

As the two doors of the library were held open, Robert walked inside and surveyed the room before him. The décor was much the same as the rest of the house, rich and expensive. There were about sixteen other people present dressed very elegantly and Robert was pleased he had thought to purchase a new wig for the occasion.

Wokingham, having seen Robert enter the room, made his way to him.

'Welcome, my good fellow,' Edward said as he placed a guiding hand onto Robert's back to manoeuvre him around the room, introducing him first to the Countess, Lady Louisa and then to his eldest daughter, Lady Caroline Wokingham, whose age, Robert surmised, was around nineteen or twenty years. Both would be considered very plain looking women but not ugly. Robert was told that the other three younger daughters were tucked up in bed in the nursery with nanny looking after them. Once this formality was over, Edward raised his hand indicating to the footman to proffer a drink, then he introduced Robert to the other guests who were staying for the duration. They included amongst others, a solicitor, an accountant and a wealthy gunsmith, all accompanied by their wives. Lord Wokingham liked to keep the company of those that could safeguard his interests apart from the pleasure he found refreshing in their friendship.

The door to the library was opened and a footman announced that dinner was about to be served. Robert found he was to escort Lady Caroline into dinner and he sat her down next to him. He found her an interesting and amusing companion, and deduced that without the looks, she had to get by with her wit and intellect. A quality not too unattractive to him. She was as fair as Isabella was dark but had a more rounded figure. She spoke of the fine life that was afforded to her as the daughter of an earl and Robert believed this to be a life he could get used to.

Yes, he thought, this is most interesting indeed. Time came for the ladies to withdraw from the dining room and leave their men folk to their brandy and cigars. The ladies were happy to settle themselves beside the fire in the drawing room.

* * *

Over the next day or two Robert had a very pleasing time. He enjoyed the company of his male companions. The days were a challenge with the stalking and hunting. He was either out riding, on a shoot of the game birds or fishing in the estate's great lake and being a competitive man, he wanted to impress wherever he could.

The ladies usually had a morning's ride and would join the gentlemen, around midday, for an outside lunch brought out to them by the staff of the house. The guests sat around the tables and the wine flowed readily.

The evenings were a pleasure. Robert enjoyed dining with the ladies, especially Lady Caroline with her future wealth and when the fairer sex retired to the withdrawing room the men would lounge around drinking and talking long into the night with the occasional game of cards. Robert realised that he had found the life that he enjoyed immensely, it felt so relaxed and free from the hustle and bustle of London.

He found the company of Lady Caroline most enjoyable, and he discovered that she was the heir to the entire estate; the family being of Scottish descent and her being the eldest daughter of the Earl would qualify her to take on this inheritance, a fact that Robert was very happy to hear. She made him laugh and she made him happy and was showing a considerable amount of attention to her handsome companion.

At the end of the first week the Earl engaged Robert in a conversation whist they were out riding.

'Robert, I wonder if you would be interested in a … little venture that I have in mind that could benefit the both of us.'

'Pray, carry on sir, you have aroused my interest.'

At last, Robert thought to himself, the Earl has finally shown his hand and my assumptions regarding his interest in me were correct. His appetite whetted, he listened with eager curiosity.

'I am proposing, Robert, a partnership with regard to moving certain valuable cargo around. I have considered this at length and feel that with your expert knowledge of shipping and the like, we could make a very lucrative enterprise. I am happy to consider the purchase of a ship or probably two for the purpose.' Robert was slightly taken aback at the speed and enormity of this proposal, but he was indeed interested in a business relationship with a very wealthy landowner and member of the aristocracy, no less. I must play this well and not show that I am too eager, Robert thought.

'This has come as a bit of a surprise to me, Edward. I would be pleased to hear more of your proposition,' Robert said, trying not to show too much enthusiasm.

I feel that I have a bit of power over this man who needs my expertise and I might have a proposition for you too, Edward my good fellow, Robert cleverly thought to himself.

'Of course, Robert my good man and we would have to discuss the details at great length,' Edward said, keeping his mind on, the other more pressing objective that could not be exposed at this point.

Robert, now feeling that he was in a strong position, thought that he would take advantage of the situation and risk asking a question that had been constantly on his mind.

'Now that we are being frank with each other, Edward, I wonder if you would oblige me as to Lady Caroline's future plans, as to. . . how shall I put it . . .

any suitors, sir?' Robert enquired.

'Why, Robert my good fellow, do I detect a little interest in my Caroline?' Wokingham chuckled. *I can't believe it's going to be much simpler than I thought.* Lord Wokingham thought and couldn't believe his ears. The men rode on and before the end of the day they were in perfect harmony as to their futures, both in business and in domestic affairs.

As quick and as easy as that. I wouldn't exactly call it blackmail, but something pretty close. More like you scratch my back, I'll scratch yours, Edward my old fellow. Robert laughed to himself. Edward had informed Robert that Lady Caroline had several interested suitors but nonetheless he would give permission for him to court her.

Robert decided he would begin the courtship of the fine Lady Caroline with immediate effect before any other gentleman, perhaps a little better placed than he, could put forward their offer of marriage and before Wokingham relinquished his enthusiasm for his shipping expertise.

So he began the courtship with a turn around the garden with either the Countess or one of the other female guests to serve as chaperone. Sometimes a ride out in the country in one of the carriages with either nanny or one of the lady's maids as company. With each passing day, Robert was finding Lady Caroline more and more desirable, especially with the possibility of a shrewd marriage and a title, to boot. There was also this wonderful estate in the country, and all the land and family pile in Scotland.

The country seat of Lord and Lady Robert Bloom. Yes, that had a nice ring to it, Robert thought to himself smugly. He could have all this plus his town house in the smartest part of London. His mind quickly raced back to the London town house and all those that inhabited it, especially Isabella.

What am I to do? How can I get rid of the wretched girl? She has been nothing but trouble ever since she arrived, getting herself with a brat and all just to trap me; that's what she did, tried to trap me. Well I sorted that out for certain, he arrogantly thought to himself. *She's not going to spoil the life that I am beginning to map out for myself. She owes it to me for having had a mother who refused my love all those years ago. I must think carefully and make plans fast.*

But, he decided, for the time being, he was having such a glorious time on the estate he didn't want to bother his mind with such nonsense. For he needed to concentrate on securing his marriage to Caroline soon.

I must get the Lady Caroline to marry me and quickly, do away with the need for any long engagement. Then her wealth will be mine. Maybe if I got her into my bed then she will be undone and no other suitor would want her. It would only need the one coupling but that would be enough to hurry the process along and I could be heir to all this. He laughed aloud, he felt such pride in his cunning scheming, *but first the lady in question needs to be seduced and quickly.*

CHAPTER 8

Berkeley Street, London

Today, the sun was shining which always made everything look a little less gloomy and Isabella felt stronger and stronger with every passing day.

'I don't know what you're made of my girl, but it is stern stuff, that's for sure,' Barbara said as they took tea together in the drawing room. Sarah had made some cakes and Barbara had brought over some scones her cook had baked.

'Oh, Barbara I do feel so much better. I thought I was about to meet my maker. But my poor, poor baby, how could it have happened so? That night seems so vague to me now, I am not sure what happened, just the awful pains, and voices, coming in and out of my head,' Isabella replied.

'Yes, my dear, nature is a strange mistress, she knows it's best to block out all that is unnecessary for us to remember. So don't think of that now. You need to be grateful that you have survived such an ordeal with your life and look forward to better things.' Barbara spoke in a motherly tone, she thought, *talk of that terrible time is best avoided.*

'I do wish Robert was here. I know that he travels and is often away on business but I do miss him a lot and right now I need him to be here with me. I do believe that he was so distressed with my losing the baby that he has taken himself off on business to get over the disappointment. But I am sure we will be wed once he is back and has recovered from his sadness,' Isabella said tearfully.

'Yes, my dear,' said Barbara, trying to hide her distaste of the man who, she knew, had taken himself off to enjoy the season at a rather grand house in the country, let alone being the one who nearly caused Isabella demise.

Barbara had wanted to keep Isabella as busy as possible so she wouldn't languish too much and fret for her devious lover. As for marriage, Barbara knew nothing could be furthest from the blackguard's mind.

It had never been his intention, hence Mrs Gates' services. She had tried to warn Isabella when she had first been told about the baby at Molly's, but Isabella wouldn't listen then and she wouldn't believe it now, but then how could she, she was here to work off a debt for her father and had no choice but to live with this awful man The poor child had a lot to learn about the ways of Robert Bloom.

'Now tomorrow, if you feel up to it, I will send my carriage to fetch you and you can come to the drapers with me and I will treat you to some cloth and get it made into a pretty gown for you,' Barbara told her young friend.

'But I can get Jack to get me some cloth from the warehouse as he normally does.'

'No,' said Barbara, ''tis better that we don't interfere with Robert's stock as he may well have accounted for it elsewhere,' Barbara quickly added.

'Yes, of course,' agreed Isabella.

Barbara had seen to it that, during her period of convalescence, Thomas, Isabella's father, had no knowledge that his daughter had been so ill, she had told him that she was otherwise disposed with a touch of the malady and would be well again soon.

Thomas had visited London only once during this time and he had sought comfort with Mary on his visit to the capital as was his usual custom.

Barbara learnt of a good many things through her faithful employee, Mary, and it suited them both well to be each other's ally in these hard times.

Mary was treated very well; she had a roof over her head, food in her belly, money, in her pocket and had access to a doctor should she need one. In return, Barbara made a healthy profit and between Mary and the other girls, she had access to all the information that she needed regarding the goings on in London and beyond.

So well-informed was she that she had actually been able to turn the tide of events on occasion, with a few, well-chosen, words via the girls into a gentleman's ears.

* * *

When the coach arrived Isabella was helped inside by Sarah, who had been allowed to accompany Isabella on the morning excursion, as a special treat for her diligent attention to her mistress. The two were taken to the coffee house, the usual meeting place and away from prying eyes.

'Mrs Barbara is so kind to allow me to come with you, miss, I do so love to get out now,' Sarah said.

With all the trips abroad in London Sarah had now accepted her facial scaring. Barbara had been a great help as she had instructed Sarah how to apply the right makeup to her face, which helped to cover the worse of it. She realised that she didn't look as bad as some of the other unfortunate victims of the disfiguring disease and she realised these people were going about their business as usual. Sarah had discovered a newfound confidence and freedom.

CHAPTER 9

The Berkshire Estate of Lord Wokingham

Robert was enjoying his time at Clayton House and the company of his newfound companions. New guests would arrive at the house then leave after a day or two, but Robert had the honour of the few that had an extended invitation to the end of the season.

It was now nearly three weeks since Robert had first set foot on the grand estate and in a short space of time so much had happened regarding important business matters. He was excited about the proposed venture and was eager to get the legal side of things tied up with Pringle, his solicitor. He also was beginning to wonder how Benson was coping in his absence. But he was reluctant to leave the hospitality of his new "benefactor" even though he did have other urgent matters to attend to, one problem being Isabella. He knew he must return to London soon, then once things were settled there he would be able to travel back to Berkshire.

But, he had still yet to seduce Caroline, which was almost impossible with so many chaperones and Robert was getting impatient. He knew Caroline had feelings for him for she blushed when he purposely brushed his hand against hers, or his person was in close proximity.

His chance arose one late afternoon when the light was fading. As the carriage was nearing the house, the nanny, who had been their chaperone for the afternoon, needing to supervise the children's supper before they were made ready for bed, excused herself as soon as they arrived outside the main doors, she scuttled away to the side entrance and out of sight.

Robert saw his chance and invited Lady Caroline to stroll around the gardens before ending their afternoon jaunt.

Caroline shammed shy hesitation as she said she felt unsure of the code of behaviour in the situation, but Robert was swift to point out that they were in full view of the house so they could surely consider themselves chaperoned.

He feigned interest in the well-kempt gardens, with rose arches and pretty climbing white hydrangea walkways. He spoke of the overhanging trees of willow, the lime trees, the master oaks and the English elms standing so majestically in command of the private grounds. It seemed he had her spellbound with his words as he slowly headed her towards the summer house, smelling the flowers, picking their pretty blossoms to place in her hair as they laughed together.

He started a game of tag and he dodged in and out of the trees and shrubs with Caroline in hot pursuit. He cleverly allowed her to nearly catch him but not quite. He manoeuvred her around to the back of the summer house where there was a door used by the servants to bring food or drink for the waiting occupants. Although there was no light to be seen inside Robert was relieved to find the building empty.

He dodged around the wicker tables and chairs, always a little out of reach. Caroline was getting out of breath, laughing and giggling, having fun. Robert decided that he was to strike. He grabbed her wrist and pulled her close to him, she, still laughing, did not resist and then found herself in his arms.

'No Robert' she said coyly as she half-heartedly turned her head away.

'Oh, yes, Caroline my love, I can't keep my hands from you. You have teased me long enough, my love. I need the reward of a kiss.' Caroline giggled, her head full of flattery.

'Oh. Robert,' she said, as he placed his lips over hers. He felt her body relax against his and felt himself stir within his breeches. She kissed him back with such enthusiasm.

What she lacks in looks she makes up for with passion, he thought. He held her close and she felt his hardness press against her. He knew the pleasure she was having as she moaned softly.

Oh, thank goodness for that. At long last, I can't believe I have had to wait so long, she thought to herself. But instead she breathlessly uttered, 'Oh, Robert, we should not be doing this.'

Robert, still with his arms around her, moved her towards the chaise longue and, still kissing her, gently guided her to lie upon it. His hand found the edge of her petticoats and he slid his hand to where he was seeking. Their breath was coming faster now and he knew they were at the point of no return. He undid his breeches and lifted himself onto her and slid gently forward. He could not contain himself any longer and, as he made his final thrust, he shuddered and cried out with the pleasure of this woman.

'I will love you forever, I promise,' Caroline, lying beneath him, made the same convulsions at the same time and gave out a cry of enjoyment of this handsome man. Robert felt totally replete.

He removed himself from Lady Caroline and, as he was straightening his clothes, was surprised not to see the blood stains he was used to seeing with his other young conquests of the past.

When she saw his surprise she laughed and quickly said, 'Horse riding, sir, that's what usually does the trick of breaking what could block your way or sometimes a gently rounded riding crop can give a girl what she needs. We maidens of the landed gentry all know a thing or two about that one.'

Caroline continued laughing and tried to hide the fact that she had just delivered Robert some exceptional untruths in the hope that he would accept this pack of lies for the reason of her lost virginity and would not discover the truth about her condition. She and the rest of her family had high hopes that Robert would now, following this coupling, accept the unborn child that she was carrying to be his.

A riding crop indeed. The very thought made her wince. *But how clever I am for thinking of such a thing*, she mused.

Robert looked out of the windows to check if their presence had been missed; not that he was in any way too troubled by this as this was his intention. Lady Caroline was now undone and he felt sure he had just secured all that he surveyed to be his.

'I thought you would never get around to that, my darling Robert, but I am so pleased that you are my first. To make one's own pleasure is one thing but now

I know the difference of the real thing and it was magnificent. When can we do it again?' Hearing these words, Robert realised that maybe they would make a good match after all.

As the coupled tidied themselves, on cue, Lady Louisa opened the servants' door and found them in a state of undress. Once she was certain that she had made her presence felt she hastened away, as if with embarrassment.

'Oh, Robert, that was my mama. I know she saw us. What are we to do?' Caroline asked the rehearsed question.

'Yes, I rather think she did,' Robert said feeling pleased. 'I had better make an honest woman of you quickly before your father gets out his pistol and challenges me to a duel,' he laughed.

That night he asked Wokingham for his daughter's hand in marriage and the two men talked late into the night discussing all manner of things regarding their business arrangements, which included the acquiring of a ship, fit for the purpose of the cargo.

Unbeknown to Robert, a month earlier Edward had found that Robert had a good business head on his shoulders. He had secretly investigated Robert's wealth and credibility in readiness for the business proposition he had in mind. At that time Edward did not quite realise the full potential and significance of this study but later, with the subsequent turn of events and the secret that had recently been disclosed to him by his daughter regarding her condition, he knew what actions had to be taken and quickly, to save the clan MacGarrett from disgrace. Edward considered that as a commoner, Robert was not the best match for his daughter but he was not a bad choice in the circumstances. He knew that a suitable member of the aristocracy would not want to rush into a marriage and a respectable courtship period would be expected. Leaving his already pregnant daughter's situation to be exposed and any marriage plans abandoned, then the bastard child would always be that of a stable lad and his family and Clan would be publicly dishonoured.

Edward consoled himself that he could always lick Bloom into shape, for he appeared to be of good business reputation. Yet still, there was something niggling in the back of his mind, but as time was of the essence he cast this aside, something that Edward could not usually be accused of. He decided he couldn't worry about that now as he could always work on that another time. So he gave his consent most readily and a dowry was discussed in depth and agreed upon. When all the deals were set and the agreements made the two men shook hands.

* * *

When Robert proposed to Lady Caroline she accepted eagerly with great happiness. Caroline made sure that she and Robert were able to steal themselves away to the summer house and indulge in each other's bodies on a good many occasions to try to help secure the deception. She then felt able to tell him with great excitement that she thought there was to be a forthcoming heir.

'Already, my love, you can tell already?'

'Why yes, Robert, a woman knows these things, we have coupled a good many times now, I would be rather surprised if we were not to have a baby with a good strong man like you,' she flattered, 'also, I have had my fortune read by one of the village girls and she has told me that I am to have a child within a year. I've already told my mother who informed me she caught us in the summer house and although she was dismayed at the time she has mellowed now especially as we are to be wed. She will arrange a wedding as soon as possible and everything will work out fine,' she lied to Robert who was elated at the news.

Robert thought himself to be a man of the world but was astonished at some of the frolics that Lady Caroline was willing to perform. He told her that he didn't think that ladies would want to do such things so willingly. To his amazement and joy she just threw back her head and laughed, 'I'm a woman first and a lady second, yer know, sir. Or ain't I?' She mimicked the local accent. She was thinking fondly of Sam the stable lad with whom she had grown up and how together they had experimented in the art of love play and whose child she was now carrying.

She hoped that Robert, being of the male gender, did not understand the timings with regard to the length it took to carry and deliver a child. Caroline only hoped that her voluptuous curves could conceal the actual month of her confinement.

* * *

When Lady Louisa next came face to face with Robert, she had to first appear to be angry and distressed at the news of a new MacGarrett arriving, especially out of wedlock but she then softened and showed her future son-in-law happiness. This happiness was genuine, for she was very much relieved the child would at least have a father.

'My darlings, you make such a lovely couple and any baby from your um... togetherness will be beautiful. We will arrange the wedding to take place soon, if that is what Caroline would wish,' she said cleverly.

Robert thought smugly, *the wedding date will be set for quite soon that's good news. I know it must have been a big event in a young girl's life, to lay with the man she loves, so I can't blame her for that. They don't want to lose me as the bridegroom now that she is undone and probably expecting my child to boot.* Lottie, as Louisa was often affectionately known, gave them an engagement ring by way of a celebratory present.

'It was my mother's ring,' she said. *Caroline will inherit it one day, anyway so it may as well be now*, she thought. The ring was made of gold with a large, red ruby that was of pigeon blood-red in quality with alternating diamonds and seed pearls accenting the centre stone. It was exquisite and fitted Caroline perfectly well. Robert could only guess at the great value of the jewel and felt a sense of pride that he had been able to furnish his betrothed with such an adornment at no cost to himself.

Robert felt pleased that his plans were coming together better than he had expected. Lord Robert Wokingham had a certain sound to it that he liked.

* * *

A small engagement celebration took place the following day amongst the visitors to the house who were still present. Their good news had lifted the whole household and all the family and guests were busy with excitement. The servants' quarters were soon buzzing with happy whispers.

Robert felt that Lady Luck was with him at last, for as fortune would have it, Wokingham's London lawyer, Mr Jenkins, was also a guest at the house at this time and he had agreed to prepare immediately the documents needed for all the business ventures that had been discussed. It was at Robert's insistence, to show a display of his good character and honourable intentions to Lady Caroline that these documents also included a spousal contract of marriage.

Although this document was not really necessary, he didn't want this opportunity of marriage to the landed gentry to slip through his fingers and he wanted the marriage papers signed as soon as possible, once his own solicitor had gone over them to safeguard his interests. He was eager to be back in London as soon as possible to discuss with Pringle his imminent marriage to the Wokingham estate. Also, and most importantly, a reshuffle of his own living arrangements in London now needed his most urgent attention.

* * *

As Robert took his leave of the estate, he bade farewell to his fiancée along with his prospective in-laws. The servants lined up for his departure, in the hope of a generous hand out of money as a reward for having looked after him so well during his stay. Robert had become aware of this custom as he had watched several of the guests leaving throughout the duration of his stay. He wanted to make a good impression on his new family and also on his servants. It was well known that a quiet word here or there into the master's ear from a loyal servant, whether it be good or bad, could cause an influence where it mattered. He also knew that if he was to rely on receiving good service from them again in the near future, he needed to make the sum quite considerable without looking too vulgar.

My plan has worked. I am to be married to a member of the aristocracy, he thought to himself, his mind filling with greed

As Robert walked to the awaiting carriage accompanied by the family, Lady Louisa whispered, 'You take great care of yourself, Robert, for if anything was to happen to you and the marriage couldn't take place, well, I would have to pass the baby off as my own, to save the scandal,' she laughed.

He boarded one of the coaches belonging to Lord Wokingham who had allowed him the use of it to travel home. He sat back and felt self-satisfied in the knowledge that this prestigious and beautiful coach as well as the rest of the estate's comforts and luxuries would someday very soon be his. He could not stop marvelling at it.

* * *

With Robert well on his way back to London, Edward Wokingham called together the few, but very necessary individuals, who, at short notice, had played their very important part in the deceit that had just taken place. He gave them all his hearty congratulations and gratitude.

The die was cast and Robert was none the wiser. Lady Caroline's name would be safe from shame and she could take over the position of Chieftain to Clan MacGarrett when the time came.

CHAPTER 10

Berkeley Street, London

As time went on Isabella's pains in her belly faded and she was feeling more like her old self. She had already begun to take up her housekeeping duties again as she busied herself with preparing for the day when Robert would return home.

She cleaned down the dresser in the kitchen and polished the silver. She and Sarah worked from the top of the house to the bottom, making it as if new.

'The master won't recognise the place when he gets home, Miss,' Sarah would laugh to her mistress on a daily basis. She knew that Isabella took great joy in doing all she could to make the house more like a home for the master's return and it was a way to distract her from pining so much for him.

Isabella had wanted to write to Robert, but Sarah advised her that it would be unwise to disclose her education. Her only hope was to visit Benson, who had been left in charge of the business and therefore best placed to be informed of the master's plans.

Why hadn't Bloom sent word to her miss via Benson? Sarah worried.

Isabella would go abroad most days and somehow she would end up at the wharf office to make her usual enquiry. It could take up to four days for a letter to reach its destination, so it would take a good few days before Benson would get a reply to any correspondence he sent to Bloom. Not that he could make any enquiry directly on Isabella's behalf as it was for strictly business purposes only, anything else would stir the master's anger.

About four weeks had passed since Robert's departure to Berkshire when Benson finally had good news for Isabella. As he saw her approach the office he jumped up, waving the letter in his hand with great excitement. Isabella had become very popular with the workers in Robert's employ; who now had the utmost regard for her,

'I have word that the master will be home any day now, Miss Isabella,' Benson informed the very excited girl.

'Oh, Benson can it be true? I don't believe it. Thank you so much, what wonderful news. I must hurry home and make some plans for his return,' she said as she turned and hurried off to tell her good news to Sarah and Bruce. Benson stared after her as she swept out of the office and down the quayside.

Good news? That is questionable, he thought to himself.

* * *

'Sarah, Sarah,' Isabella shouted loudly as she entered the house.

Sarah was always glad when she knew that the mistress was back home safely, but on hear this ran up the kitchen steps in panic.

'Oh, Miss, whatever is the matter?'

Isabella grabbed the bewildered maid by the arms and danced her around in circles whilst laughing full of glee.

'Robert is coming home, Sarah. Benson says he is coming home. Oh. I am so happy I can hardly wait.'

Sarah hadn't seen her mistress this happy for weeks.

'Oh, Miss. I'm so glad for you, really I am. Do you know the day of Master Robert's return?' asked Sarah with a face full of concern. It was always a much more contented house when the master was away and Sarah was now worried for Isabella's safety. *Miss Isabella is still unaware of the awful thing that he has done to her.*

'No, we don't know the exact day but we must start preparing for his first meal back home.' Isabella had a list of things she wanted to cook that seemed endless and she was talking so fast that she was tripping over her words with excitement.

'Miss Isabella, you are making my head spin, that you are,' Sarah joked with a giggle.

'Oh dear. I am so sorry, Sarah. But I can't wait for the master's return. I am sure that I shan't sleep tonight.'

'Yes, Miss, we will sit down and make a menu fit for a king,' Sarah said with great exaggeration, mostly for her mistress' sake than anything else. Sarah was not looking forward to Robert's return and was beginning to feel real fear, but she knew that she must carry on for her lady. She also knew that the free-and-easy household that had been afforded them during Robert's absence would have to have "order restored" as soon as he set foot over the threshold and all friendships would have to return to secret.

Later, as Isabella and Sarah settled down to concoct the menu, Bruce let himself out of the servants' door in search of Mrs Barbara. He had, clutched in his hand, a letter for her written by Sarah, bearing the news of Robert's imminent return.

Sarah had fought with her conscience about informing Barbara without the permission of her mistress but she knew that she was acting in the best interest of her poor, misguided, innocent friend.

* * *

Barbara was never hard to find and Bruce had just about caught sight of her as she arrived at the wigmaker's, before she vanished inside. He sat himself down outside on the street, with his back leaned up against the wooden shop front at the side of the window, and patiently waited for her to exit the shop. He was in luck, as Barbara was only collecting a newly refurbished hairpiece and she came out after he had only been waiting a few minutes.

'Why, hello, Bruce. What are you doing here? Do you have a message for me?' She interpreted his presence.

'Yes, Mrs Barbara,' Bruce said shyly as he handed her the correspondence. She opened and read the letter immediately while Bruce waited for any reply. Having read the contents, Barbara folded the letter again and placed it securely inside her bag.

'Thank you, Bruce. Please thank Sarah for me and tell her that I am grateful for the knowledge.'

'Yes, Mrs Barbara,' Bruce said as he sped off back to Berkeley Street and delivered the reply once Sarah had come back down the stairs to make some afternoon tea for her mistress.

CHAPTER 11

Robert was pleased that his journey was coming to an end, even though he was travelling in considerably more comfort and luxury than on his outward journey, courtesy of his prospective father-in-law.

He stretched in the carriage and thought about Isabella, she was a beauty alright. He hoped that by now she would be well and truly over her illness and would be back to good health. He knew that he had a problem that must be dealt with but not just yet.

He directed the coachman to go straight to the wharf so he could check on his business. He wanted to spend as little time there as possible.

'Good to see you Mr Bloom,' Benson said as he jumped up from his chair in the front office, he had been waiting cautiously knowing Robert could return anytime soon.

'Thank you, Benson. I have come straight here to make sure that there are no anomalies that need my urgent attention,' Robert listened to his clerk's report and once he was satisfied that Benson had carried out all transactions in accordance to his instructions, he turned on his heels. Benson stood to attention,

'I will see you tomorrow, Benson. Send Jack, immediately to my house to take word that I am back!'

'Yes, sir. Good day, sir. Thank you, Mr Bloom,' replied Benson as he sat back down in his chair thankful that the meeting had been most uneventful and congenial.

Robert then proceeded hastily to Pringle's office to seek his legal advisor's opinion on his much-prized documents, the marriage contract and the proposed business partnership with Lord Wokingham. Robert still couldn't believe his good fortune.

Inside the small, dimly lit offices of Pringle and Pendleton shelves full of leather bound books and bulging ledgers of all shapes and sizes lurked in the shadows. Robert walked over to the only well-lit area of the office and seated himself across the desk from Matthew Pringle, who appeared to always be pleased to see Mr Bloom.

Pringle knew that his client possessed an uncanny business sense that usually meant that there was little work to be done on his part except a small matter of legal advice and then submit his invoice for a rather hefty fee. Robert was not usually renowned for being the promptest of payers but he always made sure that he favoured his lawyer with early settlement, a practice handed down to him by his father, old Mr Bloom, who was the mentor to his son and turned him into the shrewd businessman that he was today.

'Good day, Pringle. I have some documents here that I want you to approve,' Robert said, as he handed the pouch over to Pringle, who was the only surviving partner of this legal establishment with Pendleton having passed away some ten years earlier.

'Good day, sir,' said the busy solicitor. He took the papers from Robert. Pringle could see that they were penned by a professional hand

'Of course, sir, but I will need some time to deliberate over these documents. Shall we make another appointment to discuss them?'

'No, Pringle, they can't wait. I would like you to quickly look over them now. They are very important to me and I need your ratification as soon as possible. I will remain here in case you have any questions or comments,' Robert commanded.

'Very well, sir, but I would prefer more time if they are as important as you say,' he meekly answered.

'Nonsense Pringle I have every faith in you man!' was the abrupt reply, so the old solicitor set about studying them, although not happy to be rushed. Robert sat opposite him in silence, giving his lawyer time to digest the contents.

As Pringle read the papers hunched over his work-laden desk, his glasses perched on the end of his nose, he had to suppress the excitement he felt. He had heard of Lord Wokingham and his fortunes and he knew that Robert's business acumen was not adverse to, what could only be coined, as dubious dealings, but he could not believe how Robert had secured such a good marriage as this for himself. After what seemed like an age and Pringle had read through the documents, he exclaimed with great joy,

'My dear fellow, this is indeed good news, Mr Bloom, yes, very good news indeed. Congratulations on your forthcoming marriage to Lady Caroline,' he said as he pushed his chair back, stood up and outstretched his hand to grasp the hand of his client who was just about to become married to an eminent member of nobility.

Robert rose and before he took the hand that had been proffered to him, asked, 'And the documents, both business and matrimonial. Does everything look in order?'

'Oh, yes, sir, they are in very good order, sir. I have scrutinised them as best I could in the time allowed me and they look perfectly in order to me, sir.'

Robert took the lawyer's hand, 'Now not a word,

Pringle, do you hear me? Not one word of any of this to leak outside these walls of yours,' Robert said most succinctly.

'Yes, sir, of course, sir, you know that you can rely on me. You always have been able to, Mr Bloom, you know that. Now with regard to these ships that you are to purchase with his Lordship, I do hope that you will allow me to assist with any legal work that may be necessary for the procurement of the vessels and to be your agent for the documentation, sir,' Matthew Pringle said, as he totted up the fees in his head that would be involved in such a purchase and along with the honour of an association with Lord Wokingham to boot.

'We shall see, Pringle, we shall see. Now, as you are satisfied that all seems in order, send a rider to Wokingham immediately and get him to wait and return forthwith the endorsed contracts. I will leave it in your capable hands, Pringle old fellow,' Robert said in a jovial tone.

'Yes, sir. Of course, sir, leave it with me,' Pringle replied as he mentally rubbed his hands together in glee. Robert turned to leave but a strange memory popped into his head. It was something that Lady Louisa had whispered, *"What if the marriage couldn't take place, well, I, would have to pass the baby off as my own, to save the scandal,"* he remembered her ladyship's words.

'One last thing, Pringle. Should Lady Caroline change her mind and not wish for the wedding to take place, for whatever reason, would this marriage contract be binding?'

'As far as I can see, the wording is such that for you, yourself, Mr Bloom, you would be in breach of contract should you wish to call off the wedding. But for Lady Caroline, well she has the option to be able to change her mind, should the need arise, sir. I am sure you will appreciate this clause, Mr Bloom. This is a fine, well-constructed document that any gentleman would be pleased to have to protect a lady. It is standard practice, but very well penned'

'Just so,' Robert said as he hurried out of the door.

CHAPTER 12

When the news arrived from the wharf that the master was back in London and soon to be on his way home, Isabella went into a panicked state of excitement and sent the whole house into chaos.

'Oh, today? But we are not ready. Quick, Sarah,' she cried.

It was now getting well into the afternoon and she and Sarah started readying for the master's return.

She instructed Bruce to get the water gently heating on the stove for his master's bath for when it would be required. Isabella was sure that he would wish to remove all the dust and dirt from a long journey in the shaky old stagecoach. She sent Bruce to the cellar to decant a good-quality wine. Isabella, herself, just ran around in a flap nagging at Sarah to come and help her choose a gown and do her hair in the soft ringlets that Robert loved so much.

'Oh, miss you go and pick out your favourite gown and if you would put the curling irons in the fire, I will get the work done down here and come up soonest. Don't worry, we will get you ready in time.' Sarah laughed at Isabella's total disarray.

Isabella rushed up the stairs and caught a glance of herself in the mirror; she stopped and took a good long look at the young girl standing there. It had been a long time since she had last seen Robert when he had given her the brooch and had said he would marry her. So much had happened to her. The sadness of losing her child, together with the excruciating pains that she had suffered due to her miscarriage. At that time she had wanted to die and almost had, but it was Sarah and Barbara who got her through, making her realise that life was worth fighting for, and they had been right after all. She fingered the locket that was forever around her neck and thought how much she missed her mother.

'I'm coming, miss, I won't be long,' Sarah shouted up the stairs and the interruption shook Isabella out of her melancholy. Isabella put the curling irons on the stand by the fire and rushed to the wardrobe and took out her favourite gown.

It was of yellow taffeta with a black-and-white underskirt with an off-the-shoulder top that showed off her figure to its best advantage. It had an air of sophistication about it that Isabella liked, and was the one that Barbara had had made for her on her first trip abroad again following her illness. Barbara had told Isabella to let Robert believe that it was an old one that she'd had repaired. All these half-lies, as Barbara would call them, were not like real ones but were necessary to keep their secrets, but Isabella sometimes feared her memory.

As she was struggling into her gown, Sarah appeared and helped to lace up the back and brushed her hair. Bruce raced into the master's bedchamber with the usual decanter full of cognac. Sarah called to him to keep an eye open for the master and to let them know as soon as he came into sight.

When the irons were hot Sarah dressed Isabella's hair with ringlets to the back of her mistress's head, pinned to fall to one side just below her right shoulder. She then used a yellow ribbon which she attached to Isabella's hair to finish off the look.

'Oh, miss you do look so lovely,' Sarah said, realising that in all of the excitement and haste she had forgotten that this was being done for the brute of a man who had hurt her lady so much. Just then Bruce let out a shout from the upstairs room from which he was keeping watch.

'Well, will someone shake me, I don't believe my eyes. The master has only gone and got himself a carriage with a crest on the door. That he has, Miss.'

Isabella and Sarah both scrambled to look out of the window just as Robert was emerging from the carriage with a coachman holding open the gilt-crested door.

'Oh, what a wonderful coach,' Sarah said in wonderment. Then she said in a panic, 'Quick, Bruce, down the back stairs to the kitchen.'

Isabella, feeling a little apprehensive, thought to herself, best foot forward.

She swallowed hard and proceeded to walk as elegantly as she could down the wide staircase. She wanted to make the best impression, but when she saw Robert enter the house she forgot all decorum and ran straight into his arms.

'Robert, my love. I have missed you so,' she began to sob. 'It has been so awful without you. How could you stay away so long?'

She could smell the dust on his clothes and in his hair but that didn't matter; she had her handsome suitor back home with her.

Robert had forgotten just how beautiful his housekeeper was. She really does look like her mother, he thought as he took the scolding as flattery.

'I am home now, my dear. I hope that I have hot water awaiting me, so I will take my leave and go and ready myself for our evening ahead,' he said as he turned and shouted for Bruce to go to help the footmen unload the baggage.

Bruce had already carried out this duty in the mews at the back of the house and had taken over from Sarah, who had been staggering up the back stairs with the water for the master's bath.

'He's home, that's for sure,' Bruce moaned to Sarah.

'This is just the start of our troubles, you mark my words, Bruce, you mark my words, I'm sorry to say,' Sarah said with strain and dismay in her voice.

Robert kissed Isabella gently on the head and as he took her hand he directed her to the library.

'You sit here, my dear. I need to bathe and refresh myself. I shall be but a trice then I am sure you have lots of news to tell me of life here in London whilst I have been away,' Robert said as he indicated for her to sit and wait for him. He did not stay to see how upset and bewildered Isabella looked as he turned and walked into the hall and closed the library door behind him.

Isabella sat down in the chair by the window. She was confused at Robert's cool attitude towards her.

I suppose he must be tired after such a long journey, she thought to herself. *Why is he acting so distant to me with just a kiss on the head? Who did he meet, whilst he was away? What did he do? Why was he away so long? Whose coach was that?* The questions came one after the other, bombarding her thoughts and clouding her mind, but she knew that it would be foolhardy to question Robert in such a manner and she needed to act a little wiser. That much she had learned, having lived with the man for the past couple of years.

I will have to play the damn waiting game and get the information out of him bit by bit or when he has a belly full of drink. I only hope that I can contain myself and keep control of my tongue, she thought to herself.

How she wished that she could run downstairs to find Sarah and Barbara. Then she could confide in her two best friends, they may even have some answers for her, especially Barbara. She hoped that Robert would stay home with her and that he wouldn't go out again this night, she hoped that he was too tired to venture abroad but she knew Robert was likely to want to meet up with Henry Brookes. Isabella was not fond of Henry as she felt that he misled Robert so. All these things were rushing through her mind at the same time and she felt impatient in her waiting.

She took two books from the shelf, one with pictures, the other for reading whilst she was waiting, but she found the picture book was easier to look at tonight for her mind was in no fit state to concentrate on any reading so she returned it to the shelf for fear of being discovered.

An hour later, Robert, having refreshed himself, re-entered the library. Isabella looked up from her picture book and, remembering some wise words from her good friend Barbara, decided to appear a little more sophisticated and calm. She did not want to look too eager, as she had acted earlier as that had got her nowhere, so she just looked up and said quietly,

'Good evening, Robert.'

Robert went over to the small table in the corner that held the decanters and poured each of them a drink. He handed one to Isabella, who had positioned herself by the fire place, and sat down opposite her as was their usual custom.

'Now, Isabella, tell me what have you been up to these last few weeks?'

'I, sir? Well this and that, you know us ladies have plenty to amuse ourselves. And what about you, sir, I pray?' Isabella was thinking hard, trying to remember Barbara's words of seduction and how to appear aloof and interesting together with the clever art of turning the tables and replying with questions of him.

'Oh. You know the usual men talk, business and the like my dear,' he parried. 'I was able to do some riding and hunting with my associates, nothing too interesting for you to bother yourself with my dear.'

Isabella couldn't contain herself any longer and asked, 'And the magnificent coach with the coat of arms, Robert? Who did that belong to? Anyone that I may have heard of?' she started to fear that she sounded like a nagging wife.

Stop it, Isabella. Stop asking so much, she scolded herself. Had she appeared a little too inquisitive, she wondered.

'I don't think so, my dear. One of the guests was travelling this way and allowed me to accompany him and take the ride for the rest of the way,' Robert lied. He was beginning to become irritated by all this questioning.

Why does this housekeeper think that she has any right to speak to me in this way? Has she forgotten her place? I am soon to be a member of the nobility, for goodness sake.

He was just about to reprimand the girl when Sarah sounded the dinner gong. Robert stood up and, in true aristocratic manner, stretched out his hand to escort her to the dining room. On doing so he was able to admire her bosom and fine figure that he had missed these last few months. He caught the faint perfume of her as they walked together to dine upon the finely laid out meal, and felt an old familiar stirring in his breeches.

'My dear, I have been away too long,' Robert proclaimed as he thought of Martha. He proceeded to assist Isabella to her seat then poured her a glass of wine. 'You look especially beautiful this evening, my love,' he admitted.

'Thank you,' Isabella said, feeling a little more reassured that maybe things could get back to normal and that it was probably the distance of time that had put a strangeness between them.

They sat enjoying the meal; they drank and chatted as if old times had returned. Robert was once again intoxicated by Isabella's beauty that was so like the woman who had once stolen his love. As the darkness closed in around them and the flickering candles made the moments feel intense and intimate, Robert looked at the woman in front of him and swept her up in his arms and took her giggling up the stairs. Once inside the door he pulled Isabella towards him and started to kiss her.

'You are so beautiful, my love. I have missed you so much these past weeks I almost went out of my mind,' Robert said.

Isabella could not believe what her ears were telling her and she felt that her fears were thankfully unfounded. Robert pushed her a little roughly onto the bed and lifted her petticoats and laid his head on her thigh. The sweet, gentle smell of her aroused him almost immediately. Her womanly scent filled his nostrils and ravaged his mind. He could feel the silky soft smoothness of her moist feminine place. Isabella was not too sure what was happening as he had never done this to her before. Yet she felt a strange yearning as Robert found the place that he was looking for, teasing her for wanting more. She groaned, she had never felt such pleasure as this before.

'Oh. Robert,' she moaned as she pushed herself closer to him, panting and asking for more. Isabella felt the ache and rise of pleasure start in her thigh and then engulf her entire being.

He felt his excitement when finally she gave out a deep groan and her whole body went into an uncontrollable shudder. He then quickly positioned himself so that he could explode as he shouted, 'I will love you forever, I promise.' They both lay totally exhausted, far too contented to move, and then fell asleep.

Isabella awoke and found that Robert had already risen, dressed and must have left for the wharf. She smiled to herself that her same darling Robert was back home again and his passion for her had seemed to have increased. She couldn't believe the pleasure that he had given her the night before and she blushed at the memory.

They hadn't discussed the loss of their baby or of their forthcoming marriage so she had it planned in her mind that she would broach the subject tonight.

* * *

Robert, having directed Bruce to fetch him a hackney, was well on his way to meet a new client at his office. It had been arranged by Benson the day before. Richard Benson is a good worker, he thought to himself. When I am away in the country, once I am wed, he will be an asset to keep my business running smoothly I'm sure. He pondered the thought happily.

Robert was eager to have Benson start the process of the procurement of the ships as was discussed with Edward Wokingham. He also knew that he would have to make the journey back to Berkshire soon or he wondered, *would Wokingham wish to visit London? Yes, that would seem more like it for the canny Scot.*

He then thought about the previous evening with Isabella and how well she had responded to his advances. Caroline has instructed me well in the art of how to really pleasure a woman, he thought to himself.

But Isabella is going to cause a problem for me in

the weeks to come; I had better think quickly about the re-arrangement in my London household.

CHAPTER 13

Isabella, still in rapture about the previous night, made her way down the stairs and found Sarah going about her duties cleaning the hearth in the drawing room. Sarah looked up and knew immediately that the master and her mistress were back on intimate terms again.

'I am so happy for you, miss,' Sarah said, a little unsure of her own honesty. It was true that Sarah was glad for Isabella's happiness, but with someone like Bloom, now that was a set of circumstances she was definitely not so sure about.

'Oh, me too, Sarah,' Isabella said as she started to whirl Sarah around in a dance. The two women laughed together and went down the stairs to the kitchen to have their usual repast. Isabella told Sarah that she hadn't had time to bring up the subject of marriage yet, but would do so tonight.

'Now that I have sadly lost the baby there will be no need to keep our marriage a secret and we will be able to have a wonderful celebration.'

Sarah looked sad as she said, 'You being Mrs

Bloom and all, will that mean that we won't be able to be such friends like this ever again?'

Isabella was horrified and put her arms around her dear friend, 'No, Sarah, it does not. Where would I be without you? You are one of my closest friends and nothing will come between us. I was brought up to value all that is good and, Sarah, that means you and Barbara and little Bruce too, of course. You all saved my life and I will never forget that. We may have to make a pretence in front of the master as he doesn't seem to understand these things, but nothing will change between us.'

'Thank you, Miss,' said a much relieve Sarah.

The day was busy, filled with excitement in preparation for dinner that evening. Isabella waited as patiently as she could for Robert's return from his day. During the afternoon she sat in the library and composed a letter to her father, but not daring to disclose to him just yet her forthcoming wedding.

Oh how exciting it would be, she pondered, *when I am able to write to my father regarding our marriage.* She wondered if Robert would journey to Wessex and formally ask for her hand in marriage, as was the custom.

Her father having sent her to be Robert's housekeeper in the first place had often spoken of his hope that she would one day become some gentleman's wife.

When she stopped her daydreaming she folded her letter and called for Bruce to take it to the post. She also had a note for Barbara to inform her that all was well and Robert had returned to her and loved her as much as ever.

When Bruce got back to the house he raced to find Isabella to give her the return message, 'Mrs Barbara said, thank you, miss and she hopes to see you soonest.'

'Thank you, Bruce,' she answered fondly. 'Now will you ask Sarah to come to my room and help me ready myself for the evening. And Bruce, when the master gets home please let me know immediately.'

'Yes, Miss, of course,' Bruce answered with a smile as he took his leave and made his way down the back stairs to the kitchen to find Sarah.

Sarah had just finished basting the meat in the oven and went to find Isabella in her bed chamber. They chose a dark green gown with a light green satin underskirt, she wore the brooch that Robert had given her on that fateful night three months ago. Which made Sarah shudder at the thought, but it was furthest from Isabella's mind and Sarah had no intention of bringing all that pain and misery back to her miss.

When Robert finally returned from his day, all

was ready for their evening ahead.

* * *

Once they had finished dining Isabella pointed to the delicate pin on her gown.

'Look Robert I'm wearing the betrothal present that you gave me. Don't you recognise it?' she laughed. *Men don't take much notice of these things*, she thought.

'Oh, yes, the brooch,' he said, as he remembered that it had been given as a token, to help ease his guilt for what was about to take place in the form of Mrs Gates.

'Well, Robert, now that I have um… lost the baby,' Isabella began with sadness in her voice, 'we don't have to keep our marriage a secret anymore, do we? So we could make some grand arrangements now?' she said, almost tripping over her words, the excitement building in her tone.

Oh, Barbara would not have advised me to behave like this, but, poosh. I'm not Barbara, she thought.

But then she was quick to add lest he thought otherwise, 'Then we can have as many babies as we want, can't we?' Robert kept his quiet and smiled at her, giving himself time to think, an old trick he had learnt whilst playing cards or clinching a difficult business deal.

'Yes, my love, we must think of all these things. Now do not worry yourself. I am rather tired tonight so how would you like to play some music for me?' Robert needed time to think and this would give him just the excuse that he needed to delay further idle chatter about any marriage to his housekeeper.

He had realised right then that to bed Isabella on any other occasion would be foolhardy, just in case she found herself in brat again and, unlike other harlots of his gentleman friends, she would not be content to just being his mistress but would want to try to trick him again into a marriage and even ruin his imminent new life in Berkshire.

After listening to Isabella play for about half-an-hour, Robert exclaimed that the gentle music had made him sleepy, he also made his excuses so as not to succumb to her charms and so he led Isabella to her own bedchamber before retiring to his own.

Yes, things would have to be rearranged one way or another, he thought.

CHAPTER 14

Wokingham Estate

Lady Caroline arose from her bed and dashed to the chamber pot that was hidden behind a screen in the corner of the room. As her stomach retched she felt as if her whole insides where going to empty themselves up through her mouth and into the receptacle in front of her.

It was July, she believed that she was well into her third or maybe her fourth month of pregnancy and she was finding it a most difficult time. She knew it had been her father's quick wits that had enabled him to find her a husband fast so as not to put her family name to shame, but they had had to work hard to secure the marriage quickly.

She thought of Sam who had eventually become the master of the horse on the estate. He had been her riding companion, best friend and more for all those years and she missed him. On finding that she was with child, her angry father had paid him to leave the estate immediately and take up life as far away as possible. Caroline, however, was in the deepest of trouble for to have a MacGarrett heir out of wedlock was unheard of and might even cause a change in the Scottish family line. She knew this was something her father was not prepared to let happen. To get rid of the child was not a consideration, as she knew he would not put her life at risk in this way. And so they had a problem that had needed careful consideration. There were many tears and shouting for it had also delayed their going home to Scotland for the season, an occurrence her father was not best pleased about.

Although, she knew she could never marry a stable lad, she thought she and Sam had something special and was rather surprised and disappointed that he hadn't bade her farewell. He had scurried off like a thief in the night and disappeared from the estate without a word. No one saw the going of him and he hadn't been seen since and she even began to wonder that perhaps her father, being a man of influence and was definitely not a man to tangle with, had arranged for someone to do away with him. But she refused to believe such an evil act of her own father.

Caroline's mother took pity on her daughter and enlisted the help of her friend and confidant, Mr Jenkins the solicitor, and between them they had softened her husband's heart.

Then together, the three worked out a plan. The plot had been set and the merchant, Robert Bloom, was best placed, according to her father to unwittingly take up the role of husband and father to the, as yet unborn, child.

* * *

Caroline grabbed once more for the pot as she threw up, what felt like her lights, into it. Surely this sickness should be gone by now, but indeed she was so grateful that during Robert's stay, she had been able to keep most of the contents of her stomach down whenever he was around.

Lady Louisa was busy writing to her friends and relations both far and near asking why she had, as yet not received their reply to the invitation that had been sent out several weeks ago, to attend the grand occasion of her daughter's wedding, she lied. She told them that it had been arranged for many a month and she needed to know if they would be attending. She knew that those living further afield would not be able to arrive in time and that would be most of the MacGarrett folk.

'I'm rather sad that our people in Scotland won't be able to get here in time. I had hoped that one day when Caroline wed we would have everyone here and make a real family occasion of things. I'm sure people will suspect that Caroline has had to get married,' she said to her husband.

'And what if they do? What can they prove? No one would dare to ask that question. She will be wed and they will think that it is Robert's child anyway. I must say it doesn't thrill me to think that the possible heir to this estate is the son or daughter of the groom who was once in our employ. No, my dear, this is Robert's child for all intents and purposes and the quicker we all get used to that idea the better and I will hear no more of this nonsense, do you hear?' Wokingham said as he marched out of the room.

The talk amongst the servants was all about Lady Caroline, her eating something that had disagreed with her.

'Eaten something that was off, my eye,' the housekeeper said to Lord Wokingham's butler.

'Yes, I know, but we are all in this together. Remember what his Lordship always says, "What happens here on the estate is nobody's business but the estate's", and I'm not breathing a word as I'm in no hurry to be finding myself a new position, even if you are. We are to keep the rest of the house in the dark and quash any unwanted rumours as quickly as possible. So you keep your lips shut my girl, you understand me. Unless you want to be out on your ear,' he said forcefully.

During the afternoon, when that morning's misery was over, Lady Caroline sat at her writing desk and composed a letter to her betrothed, as her father had instructed her. She told him that the arrangements were well underway and how excited she was for their forthcoming marriage.

The Wokinghams wanted to keep the fish hanging on the hook. Robert had no idea that her father had been the mastermind behind the whole proceedings. Caroline was rather pleased that Robert was to be the one chosen as she thought him rather good looking and they had had plenty of fun together, although there was something that she couldn't quite put her finger on and she knew that she didn't entirely trust him.

'But never to worry, my dear,' her father had told her. 'Robert may have a good business head on his shoulders but he knows nothing about the rankings of the aristocracy and peerage. He will not gain a title as he thinks he will because he does not have a title in his own right and as you, my darling, Caroline, are heiress and one day will be Clan MacGarrett Chieftain, he will have little say in any matters and your word will be sacrosanct.'

Edward had no fears that Robert would be able to treat Caroline with anything but the greatest of courtesy and respect, the Clan's faithful protectors would see to that.

Caroline smiled at her father. She recollected how he had played it so well. As well as he played the tables in London, he had boasted. Lord Wokingham wanted his wayward daughter anchored in marriage before his grandchild entered the world.

This child, whoever it was sired by, was MacGarrett by blood and was to be, by Scottish rule and law of lineage, the heir to the Dunclochlan Empire. The marriage to Robert served his Lordship and Caroline very well. Her letter read:

My Darling Robert,

I am getting so excited about our forthcoming marriage. Mother has brought in the dressmakers and I am to look alluring for you, my love. The chapel is organised with the Reverend Clegg. The obtaining of the licence will happen most easily as we are members of the aristocracy, which will mean the need to have the banns read, will be waived.

A summer wedding, my darling, how exciting.

I am missing you so much, my love and I can't wait to be your wife and I am very much looking forward to our nuptials. I wonder what I can think up for us to do to mark our first night as man and wife. I'm sure that I can think of something to make our occasion special. I can't wait to see you again.

I can confirm that I was right and I am, as I thought, with child, and you are soon to be a father. An heir. It's so amazing, my love.

You're ever loving
Caroline

She gave the letter to her maid with instructions for it to be taken by hand immediately to the footman, who was to get a rider to deliver it most quickly. She didn't want to waste any time and must get the letter to Robert as soon as she could; she knew that there wasn't a great deal of time left before the wedding was to take place. In fact it was the fastest organised wedding that she had ever heard of.

CHAPTER 15

Berkeley Street

When Bruce handed the incoming mail together with the coins left over from the postal charges to Sarah, she quickly glanced at them to see if she could make out what the letters might contain.

'Here, Sarah. Someone's only gone and put a pretty seal on this one. It arrived by special rider, right to our very door,' he handed her the letter.

Sarah noted that it bore a crest on it but was in a hand she did not recognise; it also had a pretty ribbon fixed to the seal. She knew the various bills that came by way of the post. But this hand Sarah knew was not one of those. She recalled the letter Robert had received inviting him to Berkshire for the season. That letter had had a crest engraved at the head of the paper which was the same as on the seal, she thought it looked similar.

Maybe even the same as the one on the carriage door that brought Bloom home, she thought. She quickly went to the desk drawer and carefully rifled through the papers and found the letter of invitation; luckily it had not been thrown away. She put the two together and they matched perfectly. But the handwriting on the new letter was different. Sarah hoped for Miss Isabella's sake that Robert wasn't going to disappear to Berkshire again so soon after his return as she didn't think that her lady could stand another separation.

Maybe, as Miss Isabella is due to be wed it might be an invitation for two this time. Oh. I do hope so. Staring at the unopened letter was not doing any good with all this surmising so she would have to wait until it was opened then, hopefully, it would be left lying around. She decided against telling her miss about the letter as maybe there was nothing to worry about.

That night Robert returned home tired, having taken control of the lighter men himself during the day. There had been exceptional overcrowding of vessels on the river these past days, which made the unloading of his cargo a matter of difficulty and urgency. It could take another week before the rest of the tea and cloth was safely ashore. Tonight the night watchmen were about in force, as there had been a lot of pirating abroad, taking advantage of the congestion on the water. Robert availed himself of his usual bathing and dressing procedure before descending the stairs for the evening.

After the meal Robert led Isabella into the drawing room and poured them both a brandy.

Isabella thought that Robert had been acting rather strangely after that first night home and he had escorted her to her own room for the last few nights. She could not understand why and decided to broach the subject, then maybe she could ease into the question of their marriage.

'Robert, my love are you feeling unwell and not yourself?' she enquired with concern in her voice.

'What do you mean?'

'You have seemed not yourself since your return and you hardly tell me anything of your time away. Was it a dreadful time, my love?'

Robert sat in the armchair by the window with his legs sprawled out in front of him, staring at the brandy he was swirling around in his glass. He looked up and fixed his eyes on Isabella, taking in her beauty.

'Damn, you are a beautiful woman,' Robert spoke out loud. Isabella blushed and bent her head slightly and looked over to Robert through her eyelashes. Robert lifted his glass and downed his drink and got up from his chair and strode over to her. He pulled Isabella to him and grabbed at her clothes. Isabella's heart was pounding with excitement as she had thought that his love for her had gone. He pressed his lips hard on hers, his breath was coming fast as he laid her down on the floor. He undid his breeches, and lifted her petticoats. He rode her hard until he felt the shudder entering his whole body.

'Oh, I will love you forever. I promise,' he groaned. Then he lifted her up in his arms, strode up the stairs and laid her on her own bed in her bedchamber before bidding her good night and disappearing into his own room. Isabella was a little astonished by the whole swift occurrence and saddened that he had returned her to her own room, but was glowing in the warmth of what had just happened and smiled to herself, reassured that he still loved her. After all, he had told her so.

He fell asleep quickly that night and was up early the next morning and, after a light repast, entered the library and walked over to his desk to read his mail that he had overlooked the night before.

CHAPTER 16

Berkshire

At Clayton House plans were being hurriedly put into place for the fast-approaching wedding. The great hall, drawing room and main saloon were being redecorated and white was the colour of choice, with a little gilt to embellish the mouldings and mark the grand occasion. Edward had insisted that as this was the wedding of his eldest daughter and heir to his Earldom, no expense would be spared, even in the circumstances.

To make all this happen with such speed, it meant more hands were needed to get everything ready in time and at a great financial cost to him. But he also knew that people's nature being what they were, a cheaper affair would probably make one or two eyebrows raise and suspicions would grow too eagerly as to the swiftness of the marriage.

Caroline, when not nursing the pot in her bedchamber, was busy getting fitted into her bridal gown made from the finest organza, as were her little sisters, who were to be her bridesmaids.

Her Ladyship was fussing about the catering and the bell ringing. The flowers were to be of the most delicate shades of pink and cream for the posies and their chapel was to have the communion table decorated with all manner of green foliage as was the arch above the wooden double gates at the entrance to the chapel. The favour gifts at the banquet were chosen as gentlemen's gloves and a box of ribbons for the ladies. There was excitement in abundance and Edward thought to himself that he would be rather glad when all this was over.

Wokingham had decided to avoid the chaos of his home in the throes of arranging a wedding party and leave it to the womenfolk and spend a peaceful few days at his gentlemen's club, as was his custom when staying in London, and to partake of a game or two at Barbara's gaming house. He had also decided to visit his prospective son-in-law and business partner to discuss the procurement of their ships. He wanted to get this enterprise underway as soon as possible as the connection with his friend in Virginia was turning cold.

Would that be such a bad thing? His conscience asked him.

He sent word to Robert, by special horseman, informing him of his intentions, and then prepared to set off the day after next. He hoped the information he had asked for in the letter, regarding the ships, would be made ready for him by the time that he arrived. He had requested the company of Jenkins, his good friend and lawyer, as a precautionary measure to oversee any transactions that may take place.

CHAPTER 17

Having read Caroline's letter, Robert's mind raced back to those heady days and nights he had spent in the intriguing company of the fair lady who had won his interest so intimately, and of the prospect of a title and the country seat that were to be his. He knew that he must reorganise his household soon, but he knew that in truth, he was at a loss as to how to disentangle himself from the present predicament with Isabella.

Bruce announced that the hackney was waiting without and Robert stuffed the letter into his pocket and left the house on his way to another busy day at the wharf.

Sarah, on hearing the master leave, picked up her cleaning cloth and walked into the library to look for the letter that had arrived the day before. 'It was nowhere to be seen,' she later told Bruce.

Isabella, full of joy at last night's developments, decided to visit Barbara at the coffee house that morning, so she hurriedly dressed and called to Sarah her intention of going abroad.

'It'll do you good, miss, to see Mrs Barbara. You have seemed a little off colour of late,' Sarah said to her mistress.

Isabella found Barbara and as they sat together she told her that Robert had seemed distracted over the last few days and she was afraid that he had had second thoughts about their marriage while away. However, she thought it was probably due to tiredness as he had been very busy at the docks of late, because he had told her again last night that he loved her.

'Oh, Isabella, you are a silly goose,' Barbara said affectionately. 'Now I have to tell you that I was about to send you a note to let you know that my father has been taken ill and I have been called to attend him. We have been estranged for far too long and now it may be too late. I will be leaving this afternoon for Buckinghamshire. I am not sure how long I will be away, but I have written the address for you and should you need me, please send a letter. Now, are you going to do well on your own?' Barbara worried.

'Oh, I will be fine, Barbara, don't worry about me. I have Robert and Sarah and even little Bruce. Please look after your dear father and I pray that he is soon well. I hope you will be back in time for my wedding. I will be talking to Robert about it tonight. I have decided,' Isabella said as she took the note with the address as they gave each other a hug.

'You are so dear to me, Isabella. Do take care and write to me, especially if you need me. You understand?'

'Of course and you take very good care of yourself and do not worry about me,' Isabella said as they bade each other a sad farewell.

Barbara could not help but worry about the outcome of the discussion Isabella planned to have with Robert, but she was going to be too far away to be able to help should Isabella come unstuck with the cad.

* * *

When Bruce took delivery of the incoming mail by special horseman, Sarah noticed that the letter had the same crest and seal again. She searched again in the drawer and was satisfied that it was the same style of writing as the invitation from Edward MacGarrett, Lord Wokingham. Sarah told Bruce of her discovery and they both felt an uncomfortable unease for what might be pending. Sarah and Bruce had come to know their master and did not trust him or see him with the same blinkered eyes as their mistress.

* * *

On returning home that night Robert entered the library to remove from his pocket the crumpled letter he had carried with him the whole day on his person, safe from the prying eyes of Benson and the like. He put it in the drawer of his desk for safe keeping. He noticed that another letter had arrived but written in Wokingham's hand and he hurriedly tore it open.

He took a sharp intake of breath as he checked the date of the correspondence. Realising that if Isabella remained in his house a moment longer, Edward could arrive and the possibility of marrying well, gaining the Wokingham estate and a good business venture, would be at great risk and this was something that was not going to happen, not to him, not to the great Robert Bloom.

'Isabella, where are you? I need you here in the library. Now!' he shouted.

Isabella, who was in her bedchamber having changed into her gown for the evening, stepped into the corridor and quickly moved towards the stairs and called, 'I'm just coming, my love.'

'At once. Do you hear me?' he enforced. He shouted so loud and so fiercely that Sarah dashed up the stairs from the kitchen to see what the commotion was about, she peeped through the banisters so as not to be seen. On hearing his tone Isabella ran down the stairs in total fear of what could make Robert shout so.

As she reached the bottom step, Robert indicated with his outstretched arm for her to go into the library. As she moved passed him to enter, she looked with worry at his angry face. As soon as she was inside the room, he grabbed the door knob and closed her in. Mounting the stairs, two at a time, he entered her bedchamber, found the cloth bag he was looking for and filled it with what clothes he could find lying around.

Inside the library, Isabella was speechless, not knowing what was going on, the door knob turned and Isabella gasped in fear.

The door was then pushed open and there stood Sarah, who put her finger to her lips indicating for Isabella to be quiet, she rushed over to her, 'Miss, what is going on?' she said in hushed tones.

'Oh, Sarah. I really don't know, but he is mighty angry. Do you know what I have done?' whispered Isabella with alarm in her voice.

'I'm not sure, Miss and I dare not stay beside you, for fear of making his anger worse, should he find me, here. But I do know that some letters have been coming from Berkshire and I wonder if it is to do with them, that's all that I can think of. I had better go, Miss,' Sarah whispered with unease in her voice as she rushed back to her hiding place on the kitchen stairs, staying at a close distance in case her mistress had need of her.

Isabella ran to the desk in search of the letters, but could find only one and that was from Lord Wokingham, who was informing Robert that he was to be visiting on business. *But why should this cause Robert to react so?* She wondered.

She managed to put the letter back on the desk just as Robert opened the library door.

'Out,' he demanded, pointing to the door again. She noticed the cloth bag and her cloak was in his other hand.

'Where are we going?' she asked, confused.

'Not we. Just you, Isabella, and I don't give a damn where you take yourself off to,' he said coldly. Robert's anger was more than she had ever seen before and she couldn't imagine what she had done.

'What? Why? I don't understand, Robert my love. What is afoot?'

'Robert, my love. You say to me, Robert my love? How dare you? You are of no consequence to me, madam, so I pray do not address me so. Just get out of my house, or would you rather that I picked you up and threw you out? We are done here and there is no more to be said. So go. Out. Now. And don't come back.'

'What have I done, Robert? Err, sir?' she quickly

corrected herself, 'to anger you so? I don't understand.' Her face had turned white with fear and disbelief.

'You are not required to understand. Just leave.' He walked towards the front door, opened it and threw Isabella's cloak out onto the street. Sarah was so alarmed she forgot herself and came from her hiding place. Robert, hearing Sarah come up the stairs, turned.

'And as for you, Sarah take heed or you could be following in this woman's footsteps. This household has become too slack of late and I will not have a wilful miss in my employ. Now get back down the stairs,' he ordered her.

'And, as for you, madam, you get out. Your father's debt is paid in full and you no longer have a place in this household.'

Sarah, her face full of shock and fear for herself as well as her miss went back down the stairs but stayed within hearing distance. *The man must have taken leave of his senses, he's gone mad,* she thought.

Isabella just stood there in the hall, bewildered as to what to do. This must be some silly joke, she thought to herself. *Robert would laugh in a moment. He surely would and all will be fine again.* But Robert looked so stern and no laugh was forthcoming and she realised whatever was Robert's concern he was deathly serious.

The realisation was slowly dawning on her that

she really was being ordered out of their home and, it seemed, out of his life forever. She was standing there still in a daze unable to take it all in, she didn't understand what was happening. Robert picked up the cloth bag, walked the few feet to the front door and hurled it alongside the cloak into the street.

'Why are you doing this to me, sir?' she felt confused and hurt and anguish filled her. *Doesn't he love me anymore? Where am I to go? Where am I to go at this time of night? What am I to do?* It seemed like a thousand questions were flooding her mind. Her head hurt and it began to pound. Isabella began to sob; but no tears would come. Her heart was beating so fast she thought it would leap from her chest and would truly break into tiny pieces. She swallowed hard. The distress of it was causing her breathing to become difficult. She started to take deeper and deeper breaths. She clutched at her chest as she felt that she was unable to take in enough air to live. Instinct told her to stand tall and tilt her head slightly backwards to help her gather in more air but it seemed only a small amount would make its way into her body. She gasped and clutched tighter at her chest. Her head began to spin, the room was moving around before her eyes. She felt dizzy and sick, as if she only had enough strength to take just one more, small breath. She fought to fill her aching chest, to get her breathing back under control. She made one last attempt to suck in and force some precious air into her shrunken lungs. Her head was thumping harder; her legs felt weak as if unable to support her, her eyelids began to feel heavy and with her head spinning, she just gave up and collapsed onto the floor.

Sarah heard the thud as she peeped from her hiding place and without a thought for herself ran to her mistress's side.

'Good, Sarah, I'm glad you are here. Now help me get this baggage out of my house.' Sarah looked at Robert as she choked back the tears, on the verge of saying something, but sense prevailed for anything she could say would be futile. For whatever reason Robert was determined to throw Isabella out of the house and it would be better for her miss if she were to help move her gently than leaving it to Robert, who she felt would be much more brutal.

'I'll call Bruce to help, sir. Don't you go bothering yourself with this, we will see to it.

Robert, who was standing over the unconscious Isabella, straightened himself and agreed.

'Yes, Sarah, you get the boy up here while I get ready to go out. Make sure you do the job properly mind. I want her out of here and I never want to hear her name mentioned again.' Robert shot Sarah a glance that shouted *you dare defy me girl.*

'Oh, yes, sir,' she said with a small curtsy.

'I shall not be dining here tonight. I am going abroad for some convivial company,' he said as he walked across the hall and into the library to get himself a glass of a much-required brandy. He decided that he would take a seat and rest for a while; his hands were trembling. He had never had to act like this before. He hated himself for putting Isabella through such an ordeal but he knew that he had to get rid of her, and he knew it had to be fast before Wokingham arrived. So he had to show her that he meant it, or she would have thrown herself on his mercy and he would not have been able to go through with it. *Well damn it, I do care for the girl.* He took another large gulp of his brandy. *Keep thinking of your new life as Lord Wokingham*, he tried to confirm his resolve.

Sarah knew that she would be more helpful to Isabella from inside the household than outside of it. Bruce, who had heard all the commotion as he came down the back stairs having delivered the hot water to Robert's chamber was already mounting the stairs from the kitchen and into the hall.

'Well! Will, someone shake me. My God! What has happened to the mistress?' Bruce shouted as he raced to her side.

'Shhh. Be quiet, Bruce. Just do as I tell you and do not dare to question me. Do you understand?'

'But, Sarah. The mistress. Is she dead?' he asked as he rested his hand on Isabella's shoulder and bent his cheek to her mouth to listen and feel for any breath.

'Bruce.' Sarah scolded sternly. More through fear than anything else. 'She is not dead but we must get her out onto the street before Bloom comes out of the library. Don't ask questions, just trust me. I will tell you all later,' she said in a more controlled voice.

Bruce, still puzzled and concerned, helped Sarah lift and manoeuvre the lifeless body of their mistress out of the door, down the steps and onto the street. They laid Isabella gently by the wall to give some kind of protection and rested her head on the cloth bag and placed her cloak around her in the hope that it would make her more comfortable. Sarah was at a loss to know what to do apart from what her master had told her.

'To save him a scandal. I'm surprised we didn't have to take her down the backstairs and throw her into the mews where any stray dog could get to her,' Bruce said in disgust.

'Careful, Bruce,' Sarah warned. The pair went back up the steps and glanced back at Isabella. Sarah started to cry as she rushed down to the kitchen and left Bruce to close the door on his miss.

Once Robert had steadied his nerve, he went up the stairs to change into his dress coat and collect his sword cane to take with him on his jaunt and out of the house so that he wouldn't have to bear witness to too much more of this distress.

As Bruce descended the kitchen stairs he heard the master going up the main staircase. 'He's gone up to get changed, Sarah,' Bruce told the very red-eyed house maid. Upon hearing this news Sarah was on her feet and went around trying to gather together some items that she thought might be of use to her miss. She had to get to Isabella's room to collect the piece of paper that she was hoping to find, and she had to be very quiet and not be found by the master. This took longer than anticipated, so she was only able to find the bare essentials. She headed back to the kitchen and out of the servants' door, around from the back of the building to the front of the house.

Sarah bent down at Isabella's side as the unconscious woman began to stir only to find herself lying on the cobbles outside the house. She wondered how she had got there and realised that Robert must have put her there, as if she was a piece of discarded rubbish, some worthless waste.

She groaned with despair from the hopelessness in her heart, her mind was numb, she couldn't think beyond her anguish.

'Oh, Miss, you fainted and you are outside the house. I think the master's gone mad. I haven't got long to talk, so I have managed to get some paper, a quill pen, some ink and Mrs Barbara's address in the country. You must write to her or your father. Go to the coffee house to see if they can help you there.' That was all Sarah was able to say as she pushed the writing materials into the bag, just as Robert opened the front door and started to stride down the steps. Sarah dashed to the safety of the shadows as she heard Robert address her mistress.

'You, madam, had better be gone by the time I return.' Robert was beside himself not knowing what to do. He had hoped that she would have been gone by now and he wouldn't have to witness this further. He was disgusted that she was still there, cluttering his doorstep. I should have got her out of the servants' door, he thought. He drew his foot back to kick hard at the heap on the street in front of him. Isabella whimpered as she braced herself into a ball but he took the force out of the kick as he pushed his foot into her side. He brought his foot back again as if to follow through this time, as the first time was just a warning.

Isabella quickly got to her feet, grabbed for her belongings and fled into the night.

'Good riddance that's what I say. You are no better than your mother,' he said, as he swaggered off to find himself a hackney to go to the gaming rooms and maybe find Mary or one of the other girls to have some fun with; he needed a distraction.

Sarah, in fear of being discovered, had braced herself hard up against the wall of the side of the house and as she saw Robert go past, hailing a hackney carriage, edged herself round to the front of the dwelling. She couldn't see her lady, as Isabella had run for her life into the darkness of the streets.

Sarah ran in the direction of the coffee house as she hoped that Isabella had heard her advice and headed for some sort of refuge there. She knew Barbara and Isabella were well known at the coffee house, so they would surely do something to help. Sarah hoped that she could find her there as it was a danger for both her miss and herself to be on the streets at this time of night. She was not sure that Isabella had heard her words as she had been in an awful state. Oh, my poor miss, what is going to happen, she thought. Sarah ran as far as the coffee house but her Isabella was nowhere to be seen. She peered in through the window and she opened the door and crept discreetly in and made her way to where Molly usually sat.

On seeing Sarah, Molly stood up and beckoned her over, 'It's Sarah, isn't it? What is it, is there trouble?' Molly questioned.

'Yes, Miss Molly, something terrible. My mistress has been thrown out of the house. The master is not happy for some reason and Mrs Barbara is away and I suggested that miss comes here to see if you could help her. Miss Molly, it is the worst time,' Sarah blurted out.

'Now calm yourself, Sarah. We are just about to close for the night but of course we will help. Isabella and Barbara are good friends and she is always welcome. If I see her I will get word to you. Now, you get back to the house. It's dark and not safe on the streets.'

Sarah thanked Molly and made her way back to the house of the swine who had been so cruel. She sadly realised that it was a useless task to try and find her lady in the dark of night as it would prove to be impossible. She entered the house only to find Bruce had waited for her and had decided to sleep on the floor in the kitchen to act as protector as the master had gone surely mad. Also, he was in the hope that Miss Isabella would somehow get word to them that she was well and unharmed. Sarah was pleased to see Bruce and as she told the sorry story she cried on his shoulder.

She knew he was a good lad but headstrong and no match for the master either in strength, position or wit, but it made her feel comforted for she knew he had a kind heart and he shared her fondness for Miss Isabella. They were working for a brute of the worst order and they had to be careful. Sarah wanted to protect Bruce as much as he wanted to protect her and their mistress.

That night Sarah fretted the hours away and hoped and prayed that Miss Isabella could find a place to shelter. Hopefully she had eventually gone to Molly's and was safe.

She wasn't sure why the master had acted this way but she had a feeling it was something to do with the letters that had arrived from Berkshire. In the morning she would make it her business to try and read them in the hope that she could glean some truth about what was happening in the Bloom household.

CHAPTER 18

One of London's many church clocks struck ten of the clock as Isabella wandered through the streets, not knowing where to go. The night was surprisingly full and busy and although hampered by her bag of belongings, she managed to hide in doorways and dark passages so as not to be spotted by anyone. She scurry along the road to find the next hiding place that showed its vacancy.

There were a few revellers coming back from a night at the theatre or from a time out at the local inn. People were laughing and chattering and there was a certain amount of horseplay from the young bucks out for a night's merriment. Women of the night, touting for business, glanced in Isabella's direction, only to turn away as they saw nothing to interest or threaten them. There were men and women drunk, full of gin, littering the streets and a few she chanced upon were in the grips of taking their pleasure, grunting, grabbing and groaning into the women who were there to get the money for either a roof over their head or another bottle of gin.

Alone on the streets, she realised how vulnerable she was and heard with different ears, as if for the first time, the true sounds of London. The foul smells of the night seemed to be worse than during the daylight hours with the night-soil men making their vile collections, of what the night air could belch up and onto itself, which stirred up the stench to almost breath-taking proportions.

Her head was whirling and she felt dizzy and sick, although she was well aware of the activities of a London night, she had only seen it in a fleeting glance from the safety of a conveyance on the occasions when Barbara had taken her in her carriage to the theatre or some other evening jaunt during the times when Robert was away. She could barely make sense of what was happening to her now. *Am I dreaming*, she thought to herself, and as silly as she thought it was, she actually pinched herself to make sure that this was indeed real and not some dreadful dream. She reluctantly accepted that she was in this most awful predicament. It was real and the worst living nightmare.

Robert seemed to love her no longer and she felt a loneliness that she had never felt before not even when her mother had passed away. She remembered his cruel words, "You are just like your mother." *What did that* mean? Had my father spoken of her to Robert? Otherwise, why would he say such a thing? She yearned to have her blessed mother beside her right now.

Her hand went to her locket and she held it tight as a new wave of tears and sobs racked her body again.

Robert and I were meant to be wed and have a baby. The baby. I have lost the baby. Oh, my poor baby. Had Robert found out somehow that I could not give him any more children? But surely if he had loved me he wouldn't mind as long as we had each other.

Robert had treated her with the upmost cruelty. She did not understand why, it was all beyond her.

Was it only yesterday that life seemed to be turning out so well? I was so happy and in love, Robert was in love with me, he said so. What could have gone so wrong? She tortured herself.

The same words kept running around and around in her aching, confused head. Just then a carriage drove by and splashed what felt like a pail load of muck up onto her, it hit her in the face, onto her arm and onto her beautiful gown that she had put on for the evening for Robert. The shock of the cold, wet, heavy mud seemed to shock her to her senses and she dissolved into more tears as she fell into a doorway, a crumpled bundle of sobbing human life, bag and clothes. She lay there thinking for a while and wondering what she was to do next when one of the drunken whores, together with a lust-hungry customer, came along and angrily ushered her out of her safe place so that the doorway could be used for more lucrative gains.

Isabella wandered on. She would have to put the bag down soon as it was getting heavier and heavier with each step. *Barbara, where are you? You should be here when I need you.* She walked on, dodging unwanted, inquisitive stares. She had seen the night watchman holding up his lantern as he peered into dark corners and unexposed places. In his free hand he carried a cudgel in case it was necessary to demonstrate authority to show some strength of force for the more difficult of customers.

She searched on and finally found a meagre resting place in a quiet back street in an old disused building that was falling derelict. As hard as she tried she couldn't manage to get inside the building, but it had some stone buttresses and she was able to sit against one of the larger ones and should anyone chance by she would not be easily seen. She suddenly felt too exhausted to carry on. Her fighting spirit had deserted her and a tiredness took over. She thought that she should try to sleep the night away to get through to the next day as things always seemed 'better in the light of day', encouraging words used by Sarah during the awful time of Isabella recovering from her miscarriage.

She huddled close to the wall of her newly found safe place and drew her belongings as close to her as she could. She settled her head on the cloth bag and placed her cloak over herself as a blanket; the ground felt very cold. She could hear the bell on the church clock strike the hour and she counted them one by one until it gave up its night chant at eleven of the clock. She couldn't believe that it had only been an hour since she last recalled hearing the hour strike and she was grateful to have managed to remain free from harm so far. She had no idea where she was, as she was not familiar with this part of London. *If I can just get through another hour it will be tomorrow, she thought, and things will be different in the morning, I will set about writing a letter to Barbara or my father to get help*, she thought, and remembered how her mother would tell her stories when she was trying to get her to sleep and with these happier thoughts and unbelievable tiredness, Isabella finally drifted into a light slumber.

CHAPTER 19

The girls at Mrs Barton's whore house were restless tonight, because business had been surprisingly slack and the gin plentiful, the girls giggled and teased each other.

'There's a newcomer on the streets, gals,' Nell shouted at the top of her voice. 'Come on, it's a bit miserable 'ere, let's go see this newcomer and see wha' her game is. A street walka, I be bound. Come on, gals, let's gets goin,' Nancy said as she took another swig from the bottle. The girls, all full of gin and joviality, clambered to get out of the door all at once, and spilled onto the street, laughing.

They managed to find Isabella in her hiding place.

'Wot 'ave we 'ere, ladies,' Nancy said as she tried to stand still but could only sway and stagger in front the now very startled and frightened Isabella.

'Cor, Nance, she do look right and proper, don' she?' Fran said as she also tried to stand still, but the alcohol was making it impossible.

'I'm sorry, what do you want?' Isabella said,

trying to sound unafraid.

'Ooooh. La-di bloody-da is we?' Tilly said, grabbing the bottle of gin and taking another large swallow. The girls, seeing the expensive cloak around Isabella and the bag that she had under her head, seized upon it and started to pull it out of Isabella's grasp.

'Cor. Nice bag. Wot we got inside, ducks?' Fran said, pulling at the bag.

'No, please,' protested Isabella, 'please don't take my things away. They are all I have.' They opened the bag and took out some of her clothes that Robert had stuffed inside. Nell pulled out a primrose yellow gown.

'This un will look good on me that it will,' she said as she carried on delving inside the now almost empty bag, she pulled out some other items. A new pair of boots, a present from Barbara, were pulled out and Nancy sat on the ground, took off her own well-worn grubby shoes and squeezed her feet inside them.

'Umm. Nice. Thanks. These are mine,' she giggled.

'I've got some paper with words on it with a pen an' some ink,' said Nell.

'Blimey, can you read and write or are yer just per-tendin?' Nancy jeered as they all swayed around laughing. The girls were swilling the gin and fighting for the clothes. The ink bottle with its corked top fell to the ground and smashed.

'My paper and pen!' Isabella said, 'Please, may I have them back. I need to write to my father?' At this the girls all stopped at once and all was silent as they just looked at Isabella who, realising that she had gained their attention said again, 'Please, may I?' At this the girls all looked at each in a silence which was broken by a unison of raucous cackling. Overwhelmed by the evening's events, Isabella felt her tears start down her cheeks, which, rather than attract sympathy from the girls, had the effect of making the taunting worse.

'Oh, mambey bloody pambey are we? Lady muck boo hoo,' Nancy said with menace in her voice, and walked towards Isabella, hitched up her skirts and petticoats and held them onto her hips, displaying her stockinged legs and her newly acquired laced-up ankle boots. She swayed and moved her hips about flaunting herself in front of the distraught Isabella.

'Go on, Nance,' Fran encouraged. 'Show lady muck wot we're made of.'

With this Nancy bent her knees and squatted down and urinated on the ground right in front of Isabella, whilst the other girls, who thought this a tremendous joke, whistled and catcalled to egg her on. It seemed these women knew no bounds.

In total misery Isabella drew her legs up close to her body and wrapped her arms around them as she cried into her knees. All that she had been through this evening and now this.

Just then a gang of sailors came along reeling, full of ale, and each put an arm around a drunken whore. The girls, seeing the chance to make a shilling or two, gave up their amusement of Isabella and left with the men, scooping up their prize bag and goods as they went. Isabella reached out and managed to retrieve the cloak from Nell, who was too busy flirting with her punter to notice as she walked off to make some money.

Isabella moved away from the buttress that was to be her resting place for the night, to one further down, to get away from the wet pool made by Nancy, and she curled up close in the cold comfort of her new abode.

Two straggling sailors, who had become detached from the original party of men, chanced upon Isabella and taking her for one of Mrs Barton's girls staggered over to her, ''Ere, love, take pity on a poor sailor boy. Give a man a bit of what he wants,' one of them said, while the other one, in drunken laughter, dragged her forcibly to her feet and pushed her roughly against the building. Isabella felt the pain in her back and head as he held her there and made a grab to reach up her skirts.

'No. No. Get away!' Isabella screamed.

Fortunately a night watchman had heard her cries for help and called out, 'Oi, you. Out of 'ere. Nothing for yer 'ere. The gals you want are just down there with yer other shipmates.' He pointed in the direction the other girls had gone. The sailors, propping up each other, made their way staggering down the street.

'Oh, thank you so much, sir,' Isabella said as she sat back down and hid closer against the wall, pulling her cloak even tighter around herself. The man tugged his forelock and went on his way, whistling.

Sleep was furthest from her mind for she was in total fear of what else might befall her tonight. Her head hurt where she had been pushed against the building, but she was so fatigued that she cried herself to sleep just as she heard the church clock strike twelve.

* * *

Isabella had slept through the night due to sheer exhaustion and had, thankfully, remained undisturbed. She was awoken, coughing and spluttering as she made a gasp for breath and instinctively lashed out and pushed away the gin bottle that had been stuffed into her mouth. Isabella, eyes wide and terrified, sat up with her arms and legs flaying about in alarm, and glared at the little wretch that was trying to coax her back into consciousness.

''Ere, miss, let me 'elp yer,' the little girl said. Isabella sat up and relaxed slightly. The girl was aged about nine or ten; she wore a shabby dress and had a grubby face, but which was framed with pretty but dirty blonde hair.

'Me name's Sophie, miss. I thought you were agonna, that I did. Try a little more of me gin that should 'elp warm yer. Yer not used to these streets I'm guessing,' she said as she put a none too clean hand into her pocket and pulled out a stale chunk of bread. 'You can have half, if yer like. Wots yer name?'

'My name is Isabella.'

'Oh. That's a nice name, ain't it?' Sophie exclaimed.

'Thank you for your kind offer to share your bread with me, but I don't think that I can eat anything at the moment,' Isabella said as she declined the young girl's offer of food.

'Oh, me poor love, you've been right through it, ain't yer? I can see it in yer eyes.'

At this Isabella could contain herself no longer and sobbed into the kind little girl's arms.

CHAPTER 20

Berkeley Street

The next morning after Robert's ordeal of throwing Isabella onto the streets, two visitors arrived at his front door, having first been announced earlier by a note from his Lordship.

'Bloom, my good man, it's so good to see you,' Lord Wokingham said as he entered the house and slapped Robert on the back in an affectionate greeting.

'My Lord Wokingham,' he replied as he offered his hand to shake and greet his father-in-law to be, 'Come inside, sir. I trust you had an agreeable journey. What can I offer you? A glass of something perhaps,' he said.

Jenkins, following close on Lord Wokingham's heels, entered the house but stayed silent to allow the two men their formalities. Robert showed his visitors into the library and nodded to Jenkins in acknowledgement. He indicated for them to take a seat in the burgundy chairs.

'Yes, thank you, Robert that would be excellent. Our journey here was fortunately uneventful, considering this blasted persistent rain. Jenkins here has business to attend to in London so I thought to accompany him on his journey.'

Yes, I'm here on business Edward, your business, Jenkins smiled to himself.

Wokingham continued, 'We are staying at my club as usual. We arrived there late yesterday, and after a good rest, met up with a few friends last night. So, now I am raring to go and to discuss these plans of ours. Is there any news on the procurement of the ships?' He settled in the chair nearest the fireplace and made himself comfortable. Robert walked to the small table and poured a glass of brandy for each of them.

Thank goodness you didn't arrive here last night, Robert thought.

'Yes I have my clerk Benson arranging this as we speak. It may take a while as we have a few things that we must take into consideration. There is a barque that is available, which has already been fitted out as we would require, or there is a Dutch ship that could be considered for a later date. We can either wait for the barque to arrive here, as it is on route, or we could travel to meet it at its next port of call. We can go to the office after our luncheon and have a word with Benson, who will have more up to date information. What do you think, Lord Wokingham?'

'Robert, I am to be your family, sir. Let's dispense with the polite conversation. What has happened to you, I have told you to call me Edward? And, yes, that would be an interesting meeting.'

Robert thought of his bigger investment and said, 'Now tell me, Edward, how is my beautiful bride to be?'

* * *

Wokingham and Jenkins made themselves at home and engaged in small talk regarding the forthcoming wedding and how he had escaped to London to avoid all the arrangements. They partook of the array of luncheon dishes that Sarah had brought into the library for them.

'I thought we would have an informal and comfortable lunch here and have a more formal gathering this evening. I have invited a few friends,' Robert lied. He had been thrown by Jenkins' presence as he had no idea that Wokingham would bring his solicitor with him. Robert's mind had been racing to solve the situation and he thought to invite Matthew Pringle this evening as soon as he could excuse himself and get Bruce to run a note to him.

'No, no, my good fellow. We are to dine at the club tonight. It is all arranged. I'm sure these friends of yours could dine with you on another occasion,' Wokingham said forcefully.

'Oh, of course, Edward. That would be most agreeable,' Robert replied, as he tried to conceal the annoyance and worry in his voice. Robert was a man who liked to be in control and have all possibilities protected and things were not going according to plan. 'But as Jenkins is here with you, Edward, would you permit me to bring my solicitor along to make up an even number?' Robert tried to parry politely as he didn't want to show too much suspicion in case it was to fall back on him. He was aware that the previous night's indulgence had fogged his mind and slowed down his usual quick thinking.

'Do you feel that is necessary, Robert? Do we not trust each other? Are we not family here? What's occurring? Should I be concerned?' Wokingham replied.

Do not trifle with Wokingham, Bloom. Jenkins smugly thought to himself.

'No, of course not. I am sorry I didn't mean any offence, sir,' Robert capitulated as he realised his error. *Damn the man. I am to keep on my toes here*, Robert thought as he excused himself for a moment and left the room to try to gather his thoughts. This, in turn, allowed Wokingham to enquire of Jenkins if it would be prudent to entertain the idea of Robert having his legal support present.

'Just to show willing?' Wokingham asked of his aide. Jenkins raised his eyebrows and asked who the solicitor in question was.

'No idea, I'm afraid,' was the answer. So the two men devised a signal for the other to decide if the lawyer would cause any threat.

Robert returned to the library and sat himself down after he had offered another brandy to his guests.

'Robert, just out of interest, who is your solicitor?' Lord Wokingham casually asked.

'A firm here in London, a Matthew Pringle of Pringle and Pendleton. They have been my family's solicitors for years, they were my father's and I inherited them along with the business.'

Wokingham nodded his head slowly and as he did so glanced sideways towards Jenkins who had reached for his handkerchief to blow his nose, indicating that he knew of them and knew that Matthew Pringle would prove to be no threat to the canny Jenkins.

'Very well, Robert. Let's save any bad blood here. Bring him along, man, he will be most welcome and

I'm sure he will put you at your ease,' Wokingham said with a smile.

Robert excused himself again to send Bruce with a note to Pringle who, upon receiving it, was more than happy to oblige.

After Bruce had returned and delivered Pringle's reply to Robert, he walked with heavy steps back down the stairs to the kitchen.

'Oh, Sarah, I stayed out as long as I dare, really I did. I went and asked Miss Molly if she had Mrs Barbara's father's address so that you could perhaps write to her, but said she didn't have it. I searched all over looking for Miss Isabella but there was no sign or sight of her. She's disappeared. What do you think has become of her?'

'I don't know, Bruce. But you did well today, we will keep on looking. I had hoped that maybe she'd have gone to get help from Miss Molly's. When I am able to get out I will try to find out more. But don't forget what the master said, we are not to mention her name. Well, not in his hearing anyway. I don't know how I stand a moment in that man's company. I hate him with a loathing I have never felt the like of before.'

Composing herself she carried on, 'Now sit yourself down. I have saved us some of the dishes from upstairs. We have each other, Bruce and we must keep our wits about us if we are not to be turned out onto the streets ourselves,' Sarah said, as she stretched over to give the poor lad's hand a squeeze and wiped the tears away from her own face with her apron corner.

* * *

Having finished lunch, the three men climbed into the carriage and travelled to the office at the docks where they were met by Benson and Pringle.

Inside the office introductions were made and Benson got down to business and reported on the progress of the procurement of a ship.

'Good news, gentlemen. A message arrived earlier today confirming that a ship will be here within a day or two and would be available for hire with full crew and suitable for our purposes, at a price of course, and for as long as we require it. I thought this might be a good chance to get things moving. I am unsure of the time scale that we are working to here, but I don't think that the other vessels are available for purchasing for a good few months yet. So this ship might prove to be a worthy option.'

'Well done, Benson,' Wokingham said as he looked to Jenkins who nodded his approval. He then said, 'Well, Robert, we could get this venture underway sooner than expected. Let's examine this closer, shall we? What do you say, man?'

'Yes, Edward it could serve us well,' Robert said, after a nod from Pringle who was mentally trying to work out what money would be in it for him.

'Right, Benson, we need times, dates, prices. How the ship is equipped. Do you have these to hand?' Wokingham said.

'Yes, my lord,' said the clerk, as he produced the necessary paperwork and passed them across the desk.

'The owner will be accompanying it here so a meeting can be set up. I have asked for first refusal and very importantly it is already equipped as you require.' Benson realised that no one was actually putting into words the ship's purpose.

'That sounds most agreeable. Don't you think, Robert? That gives me good reason to stay here in London and escape those wretched wedding plans of yours a little longer. Then perhaps we can travel back to Clayton House together?' Wokingham said.

Benson was the only person present who was not privy to Robert's forthcoming wedding to Lady Caroline and looked on in puzzlement.

'I beg your pardon, sir. But are congratulations in order? If I may say so, sir, you are to marry a fine young lady like Miss...'

Benson's words were cut short by Pringle, who needed to intervene in this conversation and, worried that the name of Miss Isabella was about to be uttered, pulled a handkerchief from his pocket with a flourish and employed his well-practised court room trick of a good imitation of a fit of sneezing, waving his handkerchief around grandly as he spoke between attacks to gain the room's full attention.

'A good wedding. . . Yes. Yes. Indeed, Benson, I'm sure Lord Wokingham's daughter, Lady Caroline and Mr Bloom have our hearty congratulations.' *That should put me in good stead with Bloom,* Pringle thought to himself, but this overacting did not go unnoticed by Jenkins.

'Well, I believe that concludes our meeting for the time being, gentleman. We will await further information from Benson here,' Robert said, bringing the discussions quickly to a close.

Wokingham looked to Robert, 'We will be dining at my club then, Robert. Bring Pringle with you. Seven of the clock, you know where it is.'

'Yes, sir, I shall look forward to it,' Robert said.

'Thank you, my Lord,' chirped Pringle, who was feeling rather pleased with himself and the way things were turning out.

Before leaving the offices Lord Wokingham turned to Benson, 'Get word to my home will you and let them know that my return has been delayed.'

Benson looked at Robert for permission. Robert had already noticed that Wokingham had taken on the role of senior partner rather effortlessly.

'Yes, Benson, do as his Lordship requires.'

But what is happening? What is to become of Miss Isabella? Benson wondered.

Robert first dismissed Pringle until the meeting later that evening and the other two men left the office, leaving Robert and Benson alone.

'Benson, get that barque here, as soon as you can, will you?'

'Yes, sir, I will do my best to map its course and keep you informed,' Benson replied as Robert walked from the front office into the back room and quickly closed the door behind him. He leaned back and rested his head against it, closing his eyes for a moment, deep in thought, then heaved himself off his wooden support and walked to his desk and sat down. In the solitude of the office, which was once his father's, he began to take stock of the situation.

This blasted barque not being available yet, making Wokingham stay longer than I first envisaged, is alarming to the highest degree. Where is Isabella? What if she hasn't taken me at my word and she got it into her silly little head to find her way back to the house or to the office to plead her case? She could spoil everything I have worked for. And now, Benson has been made privy to my wedding plans.

Robert felt that things were running away with him and he needed to put it all together piece by piece so that he could gain control again. He knew that Wokingham, being the Earl of Dunclochlan, was a man of distinction and used to being in command, and he had been used to getting his own way. He knew how to achieve things fast and to its best possible advantage for himself and Robert felt that he would be wise to tread carefully. For, although Wokingham seemed on the face of it, to be a congenial man, should the case arise, whether he was married to his daughter or no, Robert would be out of his depth, which was a situation that did not sit comfortably with him.

He knew he had to bring this man closer, make Wokingham trust him and that would not happen if it was discovered that he had taken up with a little tramp from Wessex. Of course, it was acceptable to have a dalliance with a serving girl, if you were a married man, but for a single man to have her live with him as a wife was a step too far, particularly when the Earl's daughter was involved.

He thought he had been as discreet as possible. He had never taken Isabella to the theatre or out to the chop shops or inns for dinner and she was only ever addressed as his housekeeper when there were others about. It was only the likes of Henry Brookes who knew he bedded her and she warmed his bed most nights, and, although Robert knew that it was sometimes just for the warmth and company, his friend Henry thought him a great stud. However, it could put an end to his wedding to Lady Caroline and, most importantly, his aristocratic future.

The current state of affairs saw Robert in defensive comportment and this off-balanced him. *I have been such a fool. Why, oh why, hadn't I consigned her, like the baggage she was, back to her father in Wessex? I have been careless acting on impulse, something that I, Robert Bloom, could not normally be accused of. And now I have sent her to roam at will. I have been a damned fool and I must urgently put things right, for my own sake.*

He decided first things first. He must remove the possibility of Wokingham ever getting wind of the situation with Isabella. He must find her and arrange passage for her back to her father, and out of harm's way. 'Benson,' he shouted through the closed door.

Benson quickly got to his feet, knocked and entered the larger office just off of his own, 'Yes, sir,' he said.

'Get me Jack as quick as you like, if not quicker,'

Robert demanded.

'Yes, sir,' said Benson as he hurried out into the docks in search of the foreman. He spotted Jack helping unload a lighter of its cargo. Leaning forward, holding onto the large capstan in front of him to save himself from falling, called down to him,

'Jack, the master wants you and quick man.'

'What is it, Benson?' Jack called as he left the unloading line and started to climb up the rusty iron ladder.

'I don't know but he is mighty anxious to see you.'

'Have I done something wrong?' a worried Jack asked. Benson shrugged his shoulders.

Jack ran across the quayside and entered the door to the office from which Benson had just come. The master's door was open and Bloom saw him arrive.

'Come in, Jack and close the door behind you,' Robert commanded. Jack did as he was told. 'I have a job for you that you must tell to no other, save the man you choose to do the task. Do you understand me?' Robert said.

Jack was relieved he wasn't in any trouble but his face paled as he nodded his head and wondered what he going to be asked to do.

'Out of your gang of men, who would you

consider to be the man of the street; who knows people and what is happening out there? Someone who could stand on his own in a fight. You know the type I mean?'

'I don't know, sir, it could be a few of 'em,' Jack replied.

'Someone who could do a good job, who doesn't mind what it is, and can keep his mouth shut. I will pay him well and you too, Jack, once the job has been completed,' Robert said, as he toyed with some coins on his desk.

Jack thought for a moment and answered, 'Billy. He would fit that requirement better than any other. Although, he is more brawn than brains, sir.'

Good thought Robert, *I need a man who might have to venture into the rougher part of London without thinking too much about it. I don't know where she might have got herself to.*

'He will do. Good man. I need him to find Isabella and let me know of her whereabouts. I will then have, um… another little job for him to do. But I will explain that once he has located her. Does he know Isabella?'

'Yes, sir, he does. I'm sure he is the one you require without a doubt, but he is not here today,' Jack's mind was racing. *He is going to do away with her, that he is.*

'Then set about it, Jack. You are free to seek this man out but, do not tell him who is requesting this of him. Do you understand? And not a word to anyone else. I need your word man,' Robert said as he tossed the few coins over the desk towards Jack

'You have my word, sir,' he said as he left the office and wondered what he could do to save the very sweet young lady, but he knew he couldn't cross Bloom.

He managed to catch himself a ride on a wagon taking goods out of the docks and was able to jump off as he was nearing Robert's house to walk the rest of the way. He took himself around to the servants' entrance through the mews. As he opened the door he saw Sarah was busy pressing the master's shirt. She was engrossed in her task as her mind was absorbed with worry for Isabella that she hadn't heard him enter and shrieked in fright to see Jack standing there, 'Oh, Jack you did give me a scare. Fair did me in, that you did. Are you after the master? For he is not at home,' she said as she set the heavy, hot iron down.

'No, Sarah, I need to speak to you and Bruce,' he said, just as Bruce came running from the cellar to see what had made Sarah give out such a scream.

'What is it Sarah. Are you alright?' Bruce asked anxiously.

'Yes, I'm fine darling, just a little surprised with Jack being here. What is it, Jack? Come and sit down. We shouldn't be disturbed just yet. Bloom is out this evening but he will be back in a couple of hours to ready himself.'

'Where is Miss Isabella?' Jack asked in a stern voice, as they seated themselves around the table in the kitchen.

Sarah quickly put her hand on Bruce's arm to stop him from blurting out anything that should not be mentioned as she said, 'I'm sorry, Jack I don't know what you mean. She has gone away for a few days. Why do you ask?'

'Sarah, I don't mean to worry you but I don't think that is the case. I think something bad has happened here,' Jack responded.

Before Sarah could stop him, Bruce exclaimed, 'You're right, Jack. The master had a temper on him last night that would set the Thames on fire and he threw Miss Isabella out on the street, with her clothes and all. She was so upset we thought that she would die right before our very eyes that we did. We have been warned by that bastard that we are not to talk about it to anyone.'

'That's enough, Bruce. Oh, Jack please don't tell on us. We would be in terrible trouble if Bloom found out that we have spoken of it,' Sarah said with great concern.

'I won't mention a word, nor must you tell about my presence here today. Now do you know where she is?'

'No. I looked for her last night at Molly's. Mrs Barbara is away and Bruce went looking for her earlier today but to no avail.'

Sarah and Bruce retold the happenings of last evening and Sarah was sobbing by the end of the account. Bruce put a comforting arm around her.

Jack put his elbow on the table and rested his chin on his hand, deep in thought then spoke, 'The master wants me to find her. Quite persistent he was. He wants to do for her it seems for some reason,' Jack said.

Sarah gasped. 'I know he is a lot of things but that's going too far, even for him.' She then remembered back to Old Mother Gates, 'Or perhaps it's not,' she admitted, with sadness in her voice.

'Well there was some meeting or other in the office today. They all got out of a carriage with a crest on it and old Pringle was there too. Something must have happened that triggered it off,' Jack said, trying to make some sense of it. 'You two mustn't say a thing.

He made me give my word and it don't sit well with me to go back on it, that's not easy for me. But I think its life or death, Sarah.'

She looked thoughtful, then said, 'Quick, come with me, as she climbed the stairs and led Jack to the desk in the library and searched for the letters that had been burning in her mind for some days now.

'These are from Berkshire, from Lord Wokingham and one other. Do you have many reading words, Jack? I've never needed to ask you before.'

'I do, Sarah. I need 'em at the docks for the paperwork there. Benson showed me how.' Together they read the letters addressed to Robert from his Lordship and from the Lady Caroline.

'So that's his game is it?' Jack said with worry, 'I have been instructed to find Billy. He knows a thing or two about street life and how to survive there. He can handle himself, can Billy, and you wouldn't want to tangle with him, that's for sure. He is to find Miss Isabella and let Bloom know of her whereabouts. My guess is he wants to do away with her and no mistake. Then he won't have anyone in the way of his plans to marry this Caroline what's-her-name.'

Sarah gasped. 'She must be Lord Wokingham's daughter. What is happening? All reason has gone from this household. The master has taken leave of his senses that he has,' she said. Before she could stop him Bruce, who had followed them to the library started to show anger

'And you just read this Caroline, she is to have a baby I bet he won't get…..'

'That's enough Bruce' Sarah quickly shouted above his voice before he could mention "Old Mother Gates." Fortunately, Jack had not realised what Bruce's next words would have been.

'Now get me right, Sarah. Let's not beat about the bush here. You and me and young Bruce here need our jobs, where would we be without 'em. But, we cannot stand by and let him do this terrible thing to Miss. But we must be canny.' He looked at Bruce, 'Do I make myself clear, Bruce? No outbursts like you did earlier or we will all be done for. Now I need your word, both of you. I will find Billy and I will have to put him in the picture and for a price he will do as I ask but not what Bloom thinks we will do. Billy dislikes him with a vengeance but, as with us, he needs to work but will be more than happy to get one over on that scheming lout. I will send him out to find our miss. We will know where she is and look after her and let her know that her life is in danger and to keep in hiding and as far away from Bloom as possible. Then we will tell Mister Bloom, that she was nowhere to be found.'

'Oh. Yes, Jack, please help us,' Sarah said with anguish in her voice.

'I will, Sarah. You leave it to me.' Jack then went on his way in search of Billy.

Sarah turned to Bruce and saw that he had tears in his eyes. She put her arm around him 'Let's get ourselves a cup of tea, Bruce, my pet, shall we? It is up to Jack now. Miss Isabella is a survivor. She has come through more than this and she will again.'

* * *

Jack finally found Billy at an ale house just off Fleet Street, one of his favoured haunts. 'Billy, here you are. I've been looking for you all over,' an exasperated Jack said.

'Hello, Jack. If you have any work for me I've been taken on with someone else. I start tomorrow, not that I'm looking forward to being a night-soil man. There's nothing else going on. I was looking for work most of the day. Did you have some work for me with Bloom?'

'Well, it is work of sorts. I do have a job for you. It is to find Miss Isabella for me. You know her, don't you? You know what she looks like.'

'Finding Miss Isabella, what kind of job is that? Who's lost her, the master?' Billy started to laugh.

'Billy, listen to me, this is deadly serious. You

must find the miss and let me know straight away. Do you hear me?'

'Yes, Jack, I hear you, but who's going to pay me? Not you I know, you've no more money than me. Come on, Jack what's this all about? I won't do a job unless I know all the facts you know that.'

'Ok, Billy, but you are not to let on that I've told you. I was sworn to secrecy. You know I keep my word, but this is serious and a man has to work it out for himself. Yes, it's Bloom wants her found, there's been some kind of trouble, that's all I can say. You find her and then report back to me. Bloom wants another little job done once you know where she is. You will be paid very well, he says.'

'Ok, Jack, I get the picture. Bloom wants me to find her and do away with her, is that it? Shame she is such a pretty little thing. I'd like a bit of money upfront for that,' Billy said holding out his hand.

'Billy, you keep your mouth shut and when you find her, you let me know first. Do I make myself clear, Billy?' Jack said as he handed over a quarter of the money Robert had given him.

'Ok, Jack don't worry. I'll find her or my name's not Billy Green,' he said as he looked at the coins that Jack had put in his hand and he smiled.

'That's just for starters, Billy. You get the rest

when you tell me where she is.'

Billy could see that he would be able to make a pretty penny. Two jobs and the day job was an easy one. Billy got up and set on his way to find Isabella.

As Jack worried if he had chosen wisely in picking Billy.

CHAPTER 21

Once Isabella had managed to compose herself with soothing words from Sophie she accepted the piece of bread that had been offered to her earlier. It was not as fresh as she would have liked but she realised that she needed to survive in her present situation. As to her future, she was unsure, but she must not think of that at the moment, she told herself, there would be time for that later; she didn't want to feel sorry for herself as that would get her nowhere. For now she had to think of her immediate predicament. After a few mouthfuls of the bread she thanked Sophie and said that she could not eat more due to her distress. *I will get used to this, I will*, she told herself.

'Now, we've got to get yer to me sister, Lucy. She will know wot to do with yer, she always sees me right, ever since our mother died three years ago, and I'm sure she will see you right too, me lady.'

'Oh, no, Sophie. I am not a lady just an ordinary person like you,' Isabella said.

'Ok then, me Bella.'

Isabella smiled and managed a small wistful laugh, 'I haven't been called that in many a year. It must be a good omen. I was happy on the estate where I was called by that name.'

'That's it, Bella. You have a good laugh. Laughing is the best kind of medicine, me Lucy always says.'

'Yes, my mother would always say that too and so did a kind person that I once knew called Mrs Price,' Isabella said.

The London streets were fast becoming alive again with people going about their daily business as the morning was no longer as new as when Sophie had first chanced upon Isabella. Still possessively clutching her bottle of gin, Sophie helped her weak, newfound friend to her feet and it was then that Isabella found the challenge of sleeping on the cold damp ground, together with her bruises were causing her some discomfort.

'Ok, me lovely, lean on me, I've got yer. It ain't far to go.'

With the aid of the sweet little girl of great understanding far past her years, Isabella managed to walk the short distance to a row of houses much like many other looking houses in that part of London. Each dwelling had a small threshold step immediately before a shabby, weathered front door which was left open with all manner of people coming and going in and out of them. The windows were dirty and the curtains, what there were of them, hung in rags.

'Come on, me Bella, here we is,' Sophie said as she helped Isabella into the entrance passage of one of the rough-looking houses. As they entered the building, two shabbily dressed young women with highly painted faces descended the stairs in front of them and in their gaiety tried to push past the slow-walking casualty.

'Here, Poll, watch out will yer,' Sophie voiced, in protection of her charge.

'Oh, sorry Soph. Didn't see yer there, love. Yer sister's been looking for yer,' said one of the women as they went out into the now bright street.

Isabella stood more upright on her own as she reached for the wall to steady herself. She had a great need to take in her surroundings and make sure that this time she was safe.

'Come on, Bella this way,' Sophie said in an excited voice. She was very pleased that she had found a friend who was in need of her help and it seemed that Bella's plight was far worse than her own, which was a refreshing change to the little girl. It gave her the feeling of benevolence, a kind of thrill that she was unaccustomed to.

They walked down the dark passageway, which smelt unpleasantly musty with the damp of mouldy timbers, and turned into a dimly lit room to the right with the same unpleasant odour. The only source of light came from a window set at the far end of the room. In the middle was a small table which had several nonmatching, well-worn chairs placed untidily around it. Scattered at the edge of the room was some sort of bedding arrangement made up of a none-too-clean, thin cloth sacking, with possibly straw, or the like stuffed into it to make it a little softer than lying directly onto the floor. These paillasses had large pieces of cloth strewn on top of them, serving as blankets. As Isabella looked around the room she saw the worn-down ends of candle stubs about the floor. There were cobwebs and dust everywhere. Sitting on one of the chairs was a girl of about Isabella's age who looked very much like Sophie, who stood up when the two entered.

'Where have you been, yer little bugger? You've 'ad me that worried. And who's that you 'ave with yer?' Lucy said.

Sophie knew that Lucy's crossness came out of worry and not malice and so she skipped up to her sister and gave her a hug.

'Oh. Luce, yer do worry so. I've brought Bella

'ere, who's in a terrible way,' Sophie said, which made Isabella feel rather uncomfortable. Sophie then proceeded to tell Lucy the details of Isabella's life story while sitting around the wonky table.

Lucy had her arm around Isabella and exclaimed for the umpteenth time, 'What a bastard that Robert is. Don't you worry, I've meet 'is type before.'

Although Isabella had been feeling still slightly enamoured of her lover of the past two years, having heard her story repeated out loud, she had to admit, if only to herself, that he did sound a bit of a blackguard, then eventually the painful truth sank in that he was worse than a blackguard and another wave of heart-breaking emptiness swept over her anew.

'Now, let's get about sorting you out a crib for the night, shall we,' Lucy said, in a well-organised fashion that made Isabella feel safe for the first time since being thrown out of Robert's house. 'We can't let you out on the streets again tonight, can we now me girl.' Lucy took control as she was obviously used to doing with her little sister. 'Here, if we get our mattresses together, Soph we can make room for the three of us, how about that?' Sophie agreed readily and Isabella was very grateful to the two sisters. 'Now 'ow about you get some rest, Bella. You look done in, me girl. Soph'll be here to make sure yer alright won't yer?'

Lucy said to her little sister.

Isabella lay down on the bed indicated to her and Sophie tucked the cover around her, and feeling safe, fell almost instantly into a more restful sleep.

Isabella was awoken by the noise of a lot of chattering and when she sat up she saw Lucy, Sophie and two other women sitting around the table which was dimly lit with candles, talking and laughing. A gin bottle was being passed from one to the other.

'There we is, yer must have been real tired, yer had a nice long sleep,' Lucy said.

For a few moments Isabella wondered where she was, then she remembered and the desperation of her situation hit her anew. As she pulled herself together she asked, 'What time is it, please?'

'It's past six, but don't worry, we have kept a little grub for yer,' Lucy replied as Sophie jumped up to help Isabella from her bed and sat her down at the table. Sophie set a wooden plate before her with some bread and a small piece of cheese. They passed the gin bottle to her and she hesitated for a moment before she lifted it to her lips and took a large swig. It wasn't brandy, but it was alcohol and that would help dull any bad memories and fears for a short while and she was grateful for that.

'Thank you,' she said, still slightly dazed by

sleep. Isabella, although not used to this way of life, was thankful for the safety of the room away from drunken harlots and worst of all the drunken men.

'We're off now, me gel,' Lucy said, 'but our Soph will be 'ere to keep yer company. You'll probably be asleep again by the time we get home, so see yer in the morning.'

Sophie went and gave Isabella a hug, 'It'll be nice, us two together. Goodbye, gals,' Sophie said as the three women closed the door behind them.

'Goodbye,' Isabella called half-heartedly after them. She hadn't been introduced to the other two girls and was not sure where they were going but she felt too preoccupied to ask. She reached for the bottle again, she needed something to help block out this mental agony that haunted her very being.

A fire had been lit in the grate and the flickering flames mesmerised her as she sat at the table next to it. Her mind was foggy and confused as she tried to work out what was happening to her. *Is this to be my home from now on?* She asked herself. It was not like anywhere she had experienced before; it was especially far removed from the safety of the estate and her family back in Wessex. She thought of Sarah and of Bruce. She had made a home with them, even if she had been misled into believing that Robert would one day give her security and make her his wife. She thought of her lost baby and how he or she could have changed her life, maybe Robert would have married her then. Her mind drifted, as often it would, to her mother. *"No better than your mother,"* Robert had said, *what did he mean?* She let out a great sob and could barely whisper, 'Oh. I do miss my mother so.'

'I knows, me poor girl. Sophie knows what it's like. I miss me mother as well. Now, you have another good old cry. Get it all out, Bella there's a good girl,' Sophie's words of wisdom soothed.

As Isabella drank she told again her sorry story to a very attentive and sympathetic Sophie. Sophie seemed to know the ways of the world far more than Isabella, even with the division of years.

The retelling was a way of healing, the little girl told her. The two sat in the twilight of the candles and fire glow and took comfort in each other's company as Sophie too had her story to tell of the happy family life that she and Lucy once had with their mother. Their father had died when Sophie was only a baby and so she never knew him. He had been a carpenter and had been involved in a terrible accident whilst fitting some timber work to a roof. Then three years ago Sophie's mother had contracted a fever that had taken her life. Lucy tried as best she could to care for them both whilst still in the home that they had shared with their mother, but eventually they were turned out when the money ran out and had to find shelter another way.

They spoke late into the night, relieved that they could unburden some of their worst nightmares to each other. Before the two fell into a drunken slumber it had been decided that Sophie would acquire for Isabella some paper and a quill pen to allow her to write to her father in Wessex and ask him to come to London and take her home. With this happy thought in mind Isabella and Sophie turned in for the night and by the time Lucy and the girls arrived back home the two had fallen into a deep sleep.

CHAPTER 22

Over the next day or two, while waiting for the ship to enter the docks of London, Lord Wokingham and Jenkins had plenty of time on their hands. Wokingham wanted to use his time to get to know Robert a little better. He realised he had some doubts about Robert's character.

All money and status orientated and sod the rest, crossed Edward's mind. It would not have been so easy to hoodwink the man into marriage with his daughter if Robert had not been motivated by the money and the hope of an earldom to boot. Edward Wokingham knew how to handle this kind of man from past experience serving as an officer in the King's Royal Navy. Before his older brother died and he had to take over the title with its responsibilities.

He needed to keep Robert close, but above all else he knew he needed to keep the upper hand, keep him relaxed, off guard and under control. He had some misgivings, but respect for the family name was important to secure Caroline's future. He also knew he would be able to sort Bloom out at a later date, somehow. Wheels within wheels.

Robert and Henry accompanied Wokingham and his solicitor to the theatre, to Barbara's gaming houses and to the various taverns London had to offer. Robert tried to be the perfect son-in-law but always with an eye out for Isabella, in case she should appear around a corner, or worse still, knock on the door. Time was going by and this made Robert worry. He needed to get his Lordship away from London and back safely into the country; he couldn't have his forthcoming marriage at risk. He had not heard back from Billy and was wondering what had happened; surely it couldn't be that hard to find a wretch such as she?

Finally word came from Benson that he had managed to arrange a berth for the ship to come alongside. The name of the barque was the Ivory Rose and she would be ready and waiting for them next morning. The time was set for eleven of the clock.

* * *

The vessel was boarded via an unsteady gangplank. The men stepped onto the main deck just as Captain Collings stepped forward to greet them.

'Welcome aboard the Ivory Rose, gentleman.

Would you care to take a small drink with me in my cabin before we begin our tour of the vessel?' the captain said.

Lord Wokingham declined the offer with a wave of his hand, 'No, thank you, we would rather get on with the inspection,' he said with slight distaste as he did have reservations about this whole venture.

He had seen from the quayside that she looked in good order and he could further see that the main deck had been well preserved. There were several men on deck carrying out the tarring and re-caulking to the deck joints.

The captain invited the men below. They followed him down the access ladder to the lower deck. Upon arriving at the bottom, Robert recoiled from the stench, shrank back and instinctively buried his nose into the frilled cuff poking out beneath his coat sleeve. The atmosphere was oppressive and Robert found it hard to breathe as the air was thick and heavy.

Even his eyes were stinging from the vapour. The vile stench of human waste hung present, despite it having been swabbed and sluiced down with a solution of strong vinegar water, the smell still lay pungent in the thick cloying air. The shackles were lying idle with their mouths gaping wide, waiting to clamp down on their next unwilling victim. The chains were ever ready to secure and hold fast in place their hostage, allowing only limited movement should the overseer feel the need arise. Robert couldn't believe what his eyes were telling him.

The wooden sills the occupants were given to use as their homes for the several weeks aboard were wet and stained. Filth still lingered. The lamps were lit as the low ceilings created little space between decks, which made visibility poor. The whole experience was most abhorrent and far worse than Robert could ever imagine. He started to retch and thought he was about to vomit. Wokingham, having experienced such confined conditions in his younger years at sea, was more understanding of the situation, although not happy about their usage.

'Yes, Robert my man, I think you have chosen wisely here. This ship will do for the purpose, until we can purchase another. What are the terms of the hire?'

Robert lifted his sleeve from his nose just enough to give an answer.

'Benson has the details, Edward. I suggest we move to the office and discuss it further.' Much to Robert's relief, he was able to go back atop, while Wokingham continued with the inspection. Once he was satisfied that the captain and his crew understood what was expected in the way of saleable cargo, they all made their way back to the office to sort out any paperwork and business was completed, leaving Wokingham and Jenkins, together with Robert and with Henry Brooks in tow, to swiftly make their journey onward to Clayton House in readiness for the wedding.

CHAPTER 23

Wokingham Estate

It was the day before the wedding and much hurrying and scurrying was taking place; the decorators had turned the huge saloon into a beauty of perfection. The existing friezes had been freshly covered with the finest gold leaf depicting the cherubs and sculptured flowers to a new excellence. The white walls were hung with drapes of the MacGarrett tartan. The chairs had been adorned with garlands and ribbons in cream and white and the large dining table had been filled with all manner of flower and candle arrangements between which the many dishes of delicacies would be positioned. Lady Louisa was most impressed by the speed at which her army of helpers excelled in getting the house into wedding order.

'Come along, Caroline,' Louisa chided, 'we need to get things done a bit quicker than this. I have an appointment with the coiffeuse in an hour to discuss the arrangements for tomorrow and I have been gracious enough to include you in these details, so please do me the courtesy of showing more interest.'

'Oh, Mama I am interested I promise. Don't be cross with me,' Caroline smiled coyly and as usual managed to twist her mother around her finger.

'Very well, darling. Now, the bride cake will take pride of place. It is made of the most moist, rich cake you like and it is to be decorated with fresh flowers from the garden. A special touch, I thought. It will be a magnificent banquet, fit for royalty,' Lady Louisa said with pride. She often congratulated herself on her choice of French chefs for the kitchens, and was never disappointed.

'Yes, Mama. Where is Robert this morning?' Caroline enquired.

'He went riding early with your father and Henry Brookes. They are to ride back to the hunting lodge as I have given strict instructions that Robert is not to set foot in the house. Not today. You need to have a final dress trial later today as you must not see yourself in the mirror tomorrow or it will bring bad luck.'

'Oh, Mama, all these superstitions, you do worry so and as for Robert not seeing me or I won't be pure, I do think it's a bit late for that, don't you?' Caroline said, as she patted her growing belly.

'We know that, young lady, but the rest of the

world are thankfully oblivious to that fact. The rest of the guests will be arriving throughout the day, so no more talk of it. And don't forget you will dance the 'Bridal Crown' after the wedding, to prove you are still a pure maiden, do you understand me, young lady?' Louisa reminded her daughter.

Caroline, about to protest, but with a look from her mother decided against it.

'Very well mama,' Caroline said resignedly.

The rest of the day went according to plan and the guests arrived at the house in small groups throughout the afternoon, which helped quite considerably as Caroline was able to sneak off and take some air whenever she felt a little bilious. Louisa was able to put it down to wedding nerves.

That night, after a long and elaborate family dinner, an excited Caroline made her way to bed in the knowledge that on the morrow she would be Mrs Robert Bloom and any oversight of a baby on its way and delivered early would be well and truly acceptable.

Some of the men found their way to the hunting lodge where they were to stay for the night, to keep Robert and Henry company in their merriment. A great deal of liquor was consumed to steady the nerves for the next day's ceremony.

'But don't drink enough to stop the old wedded

bliss, now will you Robert, my old fellow.' Henry Brookes teased.

When Robert finally climbed the stairs, aided by Henry and Philip, a new acquaintance, he was well and truly under the influence of madam brandy. Henry threw him onto the bed and pulled the cover over him.

'He'll get himself out of those clothes fast tomorrow night, I'll wager,' he said to Philip as the two men fell on the bed with booze-fuelled hilarity. They managed to stand and steady each other as they found their way to their own rooms.

* * *

Robert awoke in the middle of the night with his bed drenched in sweat. He had had a ghastly dream. He dreamt that he was standing at the wedding table with the Reverend about to pronounce them man and wife when he looked at his bride. She was holding a screaming baby and her face was that of Martha or was it Isabella? He couldn't decide.

Martha, his one true love, smiled at him, then suddenly her face began to melt and took on the structure of a sliding mass as her features fell from her face and slowly dripped onto the floor. Then the rest of her body started to melt as she thrust the screaming baby into his arms. In the dream, he could see his own shocked face and he was near to hysteria. He turned as if to run out of the church and when he looked back he saw Caroline standing wagging her finger at him, laughing and saying, "Naughty, naughty, Robert." He made a grab for her but she side stepped, he grabbed again, but she was out of reach. He was now trying hard to grasp onto her. He felt in total despair as he woke suddenly.

His clothes and hair were wringing wet, beads of perspiration covered his face and he felt so hot he was gasping for breath. He got up from his bed, opened the windows wide and stood there, his hand on the wall to steady himself, trying to cool down and get the vision from his mind. The cool night air made the wet on his clothes turn cold, but at least he could breathe again. He removed his breeches and stockings with difficulty, his waistcoat and shirt clung stickily to his body. He poured some cold water into the bowl on the wash stand and sponged himself down. He then put on some clean dry night clothes and went in search of Henry, for some sort of comfort from his friend and confidant.

Henry and Robert joked that they knew all things about each other which was enough for them both to swing at 'Old Tyburn', laughing at the reference to the gallows old location.

He found Henry asleep and woke him, telling him of the nightmare he had just endured. Henry, who was still suffering from the overdose of alcohol, was groggy and none too pleased at being disturbed at this hour but, being the good and usually calm-natured friend that he was, laughed heartily at the distress of his best friend.

'My dear man, you are on the eve of your wedding and marriage to the lovely Caroline, who is heir to the Wokingham estate. I should imagine you would have such a dream. In fact I'm rather surprised it was such a mild vision that bothered you so. Now, my dear fellow, back to bed with you and back to sleep. What nonsense you have rolling around in that head of yours. You will be fit for nothing in the morning if you don't get yourself to sleep right now. And come to that neither will I,' he teased, as he laughingly sent Robert off down the corridor back to his own room.

* * *

The next morning there was much joviality and all was calm again in Robert's mind. Henry's wise words had set his mind at rest, especially with mention of the inheritance of the Wokingham estate.

The men ate a small breakfast before their valet de chambre powdered their wigs and assisted them to dress for the ceremony. The men then went into the long hall of the hunting lodge and waited for the time to come for them to make their way to the chapel. Lord Wokingham, who had also stayed at the lodge, mainly to get out of the way of the women, had ridden in his carriage, proud in his kilt, to the main house to check that all was well with his visiting guests.

At Clayton House there was all the fuss and pomp of any aristocratic family with a wedding happening that day.

The bagpipers were playing to call in all good fortune for the coming event.

Guests would meet in corridors of the grand house and nod to each other or, if more familiar, throw their arms about each other in greeting, some with half-eaten food in their hands as they hurried from the early dawn breakfast to get their coiffeur done or their wedding costumes on. Guests were bellowing for their maids to come and assist them getting into tight-fitting or awkward garments. Voices were distraught and raised. The gentlemen shouted for their valets to arrange their attire and powder their wigs. There was a noise and commotion almost as loud as a London market on a sunny day.

Safe in her room, Caroline waited patiently in her bed, not wanting to stir just yet. She, could think of little else than the disgrace she could have brought upon her family. She had been brought up to shoulder her responsibility well and be head of a highly-respected dynasty. But now, as she lay there, she started to wonder about this man she was to marry. What was her life to be like? Her thoughts turned to Sam. She knew that she really loved him, but knew they could never marry.

So much for love, she thought to herself, *at least with Robert it would be a marriage of a certain understanding. Father must have chosen him particularly well for a purpose, even though he's not of the same social standing as I, he isn't of the serving classes, I suppose.*

But at least she had her little baby to remind her of her lost love and there would be an heir to carry on the clan MacGarrett. She did not care for Robert enough to want to have his child and it was with cunning that the family had hoodwinked him into believing this child was his.

A riding crop indeed! Whatever next, Caroline thought to herself with a giggle. Just then her maid knocked on the door and brought her the dry bread and cup of tea that usually helped her mistress rise each morning without the need to head straight for the bowl in the corner of the room.

Fortunately, today the morning ritual did the trick and Caroline was able to get from her bed and bathe without the unnecessary worry of the morning sickness.

The maid helped her into the blue gown the dressmaker had made in haste to meet the wedding date. The tartan sash was fixed from one shoulder diagonally across her bodice and hung nearly to the floor. Her hair had been coiled and teased into a glorious style to fit the occasion.

Caroline, with her bridesmaids in attendance, descended the stairs. Louisa had tears welling in her eyes as she looked at her beautiful daughter.

'My darling. How beautiful you look on your wedding day. The carriage is ready for us darling, good luck,' she said, as they walked through the highly decorated open door and into the garland-decorated coach to take them the short distance to the chapel on the estate.

* * *

The ceremony went according to plan and there was no sighting of anything in Robert's dream.

Henry was the first to congratulate his dear friend as the congregation exited the chapel, 'You see, Robert my old fellow, I sent all those nasty worries and dreams away for you.' He laughed most heartily as he took Robert's hand and shook it with great gusto. 'Well done, Robert my friend, congratulations,' he continued.

Robert was indeed a most happy fellow; people were shaking his hand and slapping him upon the back in merriment and salutations to him and his bride, as he climbed up into the carriage beside Lady Caroline, his wife. They rode the short distance from the chapel to the house for the wedding feast. With the house in view he thought, one day this will be my house.

All was going as he had intended and soon he would be back in London to take up his new enterprise with his father-in-law. Robert could not believe life could be so sweet for him after that disastrous episode with Isabella.

Lady Caroline sat beside her husband, overwhelmed by the emotion of the events. *So what if Robert is not the best catch, at least the baby will have a name and will now be born in wedlock and then, Lady Caroline told herself, when all the dust has settled and everyone has finished billing and cooing over my baby, I will find a way to* end my marriage to Mr Bloom. Father has told me "wheels within wheels, my dear." And she had every faith that she would not have to spend the rest of her life with this upstart.

She glanced sideways at Robert, and smiled; as

good looking as he was, she could see right through him. But for now he would make a handsome diversion.

CHAPTER 24

London

For the price of a few swigs of gin, Sophie was able to obtain from a street girl some writing paper, which she hurriedly took back to Isabella. Sophie found her sitting by the remaining embers of last night's fire.

Isabella, although grateful for her refuge in the small but friendly household, was unaccustomed to sleeping in such rough conditions. Her memory of the first night out on the cold London streets was too much for her to think about; she still bore the faint signs of the bruises from her ordeal and she feared that her body had taken a chill as she cuddled closer to the fire and shivered in the cold, dank room.

''Ere, Bella I 'ave some lov-er-ly paper for yer to write to yer papa,' a very excited Sophie chirped as she rushed to sit beside Isabella.

'Sophie, thank you so much,' she said, 'I was sitting here getting very home-sick for Wessex. I do miss my father so,' Isabella said as she gratefully took the precious gift from the little girl's outstretched hand and gave her a hug.

'And I have a quill for yer, it's not best but it'll do yer, 'ere is some ink and sealing wax as well. I kinda borrowed um from the landlady some months back,' Sophie offered.

'Did she know that you had them?' Isabella enquired.

'Na, 'corse not. Don't be daft,' Sophie said and Isabella couldn't help but chuckle. Sophie laughed realising that she wasn't in any trouble. She was beginning to feel a very close bond with Isabella.

'I must set about writing to my father straight away. Will you be able to take it to the inn for the posting for me, Sophie?'

''Corse I can me lovely. 'Ere what's yer last name again, Bella?'

Isabella hesitated a moment as she had to think. These past two years she had always thought of herself as Bloom. She concentrated to remember her name, 'Um, it's Walker, the same as my father,' she replied.

Sophie laid down on her bed to rest while Isabella wrote to her father.

27 Berwick Street
London
 Dear Father,

It is with great regret that I write to inform you that I no longer reside at the Bloom residence in Berkeley Street. I do not wish to alarm you but I feel that I have brought shame upon the family for Mr Bloom discharged me at a moment's notice and told me that your debt to him had been paid in full. Although I am glad that you are no longer under obligation to him, I would have hoped that he would have allowed me the means by which I could have returned home.

Barbara Newman is away in the country at this time of writing or I am sure she would have afforded me the necessary funds to purchase a passage on the coach.

I am sorry to have to ask but would it be possible on your next excursion into London, that you might collect me to take me home to Wessex with you?

Please, Father, I beg that you send word to my new address upon receipt of this correspondence to you. Please reassure me that you have forgiven me and I have not disgraced you in anyway and that you are willing and able to come for me.

Please, Father, I beg that you let me know soonest that you hold no ill will against me and give me news of when my return home is likely to take place.

Please send post-paid as I don't quite have the funds to pay for your letter to me.

I await your earliest reply,
Your ever loving daughter.
Isabella

As Isabella finished writing the letter her eyes filled with tears. She carefully folded the paper and addressed it to her father. Using the wax she had melted in the flame of a candle, she sealed the letter.

'Sophie, would you be kind and take this letter to the inn keeper for it to travel on the next mail coach, as fast as you can, my little one,' Isabella said to the quietly waiting little girl.

''Corse, me lovely,' Sophie replied eagerly. Jumping from her bed she took the letter in her hand and looked at the words written upon it, ''Ere, what's that? Is it yer father's name in those words?' she asked.

'Yes, Sophie it is. I could teach you to read a few words, while I still am here, if you would like.' Isabella replied.

'Yes, please me Bella, I'd really like that.'

Sophie left the house and made her way to the staging post to catch the next coach bound for Wessex. She skipped along the streets, greeting and laughingly dodging around the many street hawkers and broad sheet sellers who she knew along the way. Having no mother or father, and with her sister Lucy either out working or having fun with the older girls, Sophie felt lonely most of the time but at last she had found someone to love and look after her or maybe it was the other way round, she thought. She wondered if Isabella would allow her to go with her back to Wessex.

'I'll ask her. I know she'll say yes,' she said to herself out loud as she lifted the skirt of her dress that had seen better days, to jump a puddle in the cold morning air. Sophie felt so happy to have Isabella in her life, she stopped by a brazier to warm her hands and smiled as she watched the dancing flames.

'Hello, Mo,' Sophie said to a street vendor. 'I'm gunna live in Wessex, I is, with me friend Bella.'

'Are yer, Soph? Yeah, 'corse yer is, darling. She'll want the likes of you with 'er won't she,' Mo mocked with a laugh.

Sophie looked at Mo. Well, that ain't nice, why would she fink that? She just don't blimin believe me, the old cow. Sophie looked at Mo with a scowl on her face.

* * *

In the days that followed Isabella's bruises and sores cleared and she busied herself with cleaning and tidying the room and making meals for the girls with the little food that was available. She felt that she was making her contribution to the work force and would not be seen as slacking to the rest of her household. In fact, the room took on a new look as the beds were put away when not in use. She had learnt from Sophie the names of the girls and how they all made their money. She felt saddened that life in London was so cruel.

Ellen would wash out her sheep gut skin that she used to protect herself from unwanted babies. While Josie, having lost her child, continued to be a wet nurse to those better off and who could afford her, which served as a way of income and also, she believed, as a preventative against her falling with child again. The girls would work different shifts, as men's appetites had no routine hours, although the night shift saw more of a lucrative time as the men found more of a lust after a drink or two. It was also easier for the girls to pickpocket in the dim light than during the daylight hours.

So Isabella worked when she could around the sleeping girls trying not to disturb them.

It was well into the third week and her father hadn't answered her letter and she felt sure that he would have replied immediately to reassure her of his intention to collect her. Isabella was getting more and more distressed by this lack of contact and feared that her father may not have forgiven her or maybe he had thought that she had done something to cause Robert to dismiss her in such a fashion. She confided in Sophie, who was her constant companion.

'Don't be daft, Bella,' little Sophie said as she helped Isabella put the beds away into the corner. 'I'm sure he is just busy. That's all, lovely.'

Isabella didn't feel quite so convinced, but all she could do was wait. It can't be much longer she, thought to herself.

Then late one morning Isabella walked into the room and found the girls in a huddle. They all turned and looked at her in such a way that made her feel uncomfortable.

Lucy stood up and looked at Isabella, 'Look, Bella, we all like yer 'ere yer know that don't cha? And we knows you is doing yer best in the circumstances.' She then put her hands on her hips and her tone changed and took on an angry note and she started to speak quicker and with a toss of her head she continued, 'But you haven't given much to us gels here, 'ave yer? We go out and bring in the food and the money and all you's do is a bit of sweepin'. Well, you gotta put in the pot, you 'ave and get out there. We can't keep yer in food and rent forever, yer know.'

'Yeah, Lady Bella. We ain't yer servants yer knows like in yer big 'ouse you're always talking about,' scorned Ellen.

Isabella was so taken aback with the ferocity and so astonished at this sudden verbal attack that she turned quite pale. Not in her wildest dreams did she think this had been going on in the girls' minds. Sophie, who had walked into the room close behind Isabella, stood listening with her mouth open. In dismay she ran at her sister and beat her with her fists.

'You take that back, Luce, you old cow,' she cried.

Isabella ran over to take the screaming and kicking Sophie off of her sister, 'No, Sophie, your sister is right. Oh, Lucy why didn't you say something before? I am so sorry. I was sure that my father would have written with word to me by now, and I would have been out of your way,' Isabella said as she calmed Sophie by stroking her hair. 'What can I do to help? I don't know what I can do?'

Ellen stood up, 'Well, don't cha now, well the same as we have to do to get ourselves by, that's wot.'

'What? I don't understand. You mean by being a, um...' Isabella quickly corrected herself, 'work on the streets, you mean?' She didn't want to sound judgemental as she knew that given a choice this was the last thing the girls would choose, so she quickly continued, 'I don't know if I could, I know that you do but I am so afraid, you are braver than me.' Even then it didn't sound very understanding, in fact it appeared as if she was looking down her nose at them and her eyes teared.

'I know,' Lucy said a little more compassionately as she came over to her and put her arm around her. 'Yer have been through a lot but we need to make ends meet 'ere and yer an extra mouth ta feed. Look, we'll help yer. It'll be easier than it sounds and a good-looking gel like you will fetch a pretty penny. Yer'll have us all dining out on champagne in no time.' She laughed.

Isabella looked at Lucy and knew that she had to find a new strength; if she wanted to survive this world she had to do as they did. It would only be until her father came to collect her. Oh, Father, she thought, *it will have to be my secret as you would be devastated, father, if you thought that I had become a. . . lady of the night.* Mrs Price would never understand it or even believe it of her and would be horrified; she wondered if Mrs Price even knew that such ladies even existed and another tear welled in her eyes.

It had been agreed amongst the girls that Isabella should get her first night over with as soon as possible. While the others readied themselves for the night ahead, Lucy sat Isabella down and told her a few invaluable things to get her through the night ahead.

'Right, me girl,' Lucy said in a motherly tone that she usually reserved for Sophie. 'Number one, you don't go anywhere alone. Two, you make sure that one of the other girls is in full sight at all times. Three, yer don't have to do anything yer really don't wanna do and four, above all else – get their bloody money first or the sods will run off and not pay yer. All it is really is wot you gave away for free when yer were in love, you now give it away for money, me lovely, that's all it is. And remember you can run faster with yer skirts up than he can with his breeches down,' she laughed.

Lucy had remembered that Isabella had told her that due to her miscarriage she was unable to have babies so getting pregnant wouldn't be a concern for

Isabella and Lucy didn't want say this and remind her of her past life with Bloom.

'Yer first time will be yer worst,' Ellen said as if in some way to console her.

'That's it. Make her feel worse, why don't yer?' Lucy scolded.

'Oh, no, I didn't mean to upset yer. Just let's get it out the way and then it will be easy next time,' she said feeling rather bad, ''Ere let's do yer hair for yer,' she offered trying to make amends.

'Alright, please I need all the help I can get.' Isabella said very nervously, not quite sure that she wanted to look her best for such an occasion as this.

'Give her another swig of that gin someone, will yer?' Lucy said. 'Come on, Bella, you will be fine, yer know that, don't cha? We'll all be with yer we won't leave yer on yer own,' Lucy reassured.

'Yeah. We'll all be there, we all had to have a first time, yer know,' Josie said, as she found some red powder to paint onto Isabella's trembling lips and rub some onto her now very pale cheeks.

'Well, I fink yer's all horrid, I does, making me Bella go out to do this when she ain't used to it,' Sophie said as she sat hugging her knees in the corner of the room. She had had strict instructions to stay out of the way and sleep until the girls returned in the early morning. Sophie had got used to Isabella being there at night and she not only worried for her friend but she didn't much want to spend the nights alone again since Isabella had come to live with them.

Lucy had given Isabella one of her own bodice's together with one of her skirt's to wear for the night. Isabella had said that she couldn't bring herself to alter her own clothes into such a style. "I will need something to wear when my father comes for me and I can't have him see me dressed like this," she had pleaded.

'Well, we's all set then, girls. Off we go,' Lucy said, as she linked arms with Isabella.

As they walked up the hall Isabella caught sight of herself in the large cracked and scruffy mirror on the wall and gasped. She thought she was looking at Josie's reflection at first and then she realised that it was her own. Her hair had been piled up on top with some tumbling strands that had fallen out. Her lips and cheeks were scarlet red and she had a black spot painted just below her right eye. The bodice was low cut and revealed a lot more than Isabella wanted to show to these strangers. Come on, Isabella, she told herself, you have survived more than this.

'You look luv-ver-ly, Bella. One look a' yer and the poor gentleman will 'ave it all over in a trice before 'e 'as time to unbutton 'is breeches. Now, best foot forward, Bella,' Ellen said.

'Oh, please. Which one is that?' Isabella said without thinking, which made them laugh, including Isabella herself, which helped to relieve the tension just a little. They all tipped out into the street and as they passed the gin bottle around they made sure that Isabella got more than her fair share to help ease her worries. What am I doing? Isabella thought to herself. Her mother entered her mind but she thought ashamedly, *no, mother, you can't come here with me tonight, I have to do this alone.*

Sophie had gone to the door and looked after them and hoped that Isabella would be back home again soon, safe and sound.

The girls walked along the streets, arm-in-arm with Isabella, as they tried to make merriment to try to make less of the event. Although, Isabella had had quite a lot to drink it didn't seem to have any effect on her; she really wished that it would produce the required mindlessness soon, so that she could perform the tasks ahead.

They turned down Old Compton Street still in linked arms and found themselves a group of doorways to stand beside.

''Ere Bella, you stand there and a nice gent will

come along any minute and take a fancy to yer. Now don't forget, money first,' Lucy said.

Isabella stood where she had been instructed, she was shaking and her head was spinning from fear and her heart was beating faster than she thought it could. She felt that she was going to faint, but willed herself to stand her ground, just as a man approached her. *Oh, no, she thought, this is much too soon. I need time to get settled standing here first.*

Ellen looked at Lucy and made a gesture with her hand with pointed thumb in Isabella direction and whispered, 'She'll be alright, she's gone and got a nice gent here.'

'Hello, my girl. How much?' the gentleman asked.

She had been told to ask what it was he wanted and price it accordingly, but in her distressed state she blurted out, 'a shilling, money first.'

'What! A shilling! Well you look a pretty one. I've not seen you here before. You had better show me what you can do for me for a shilling,' he said as he put his hand in his pocket and produced the required amount of money, then made a grab for the shaking Isabella and kissed her full on the mouth and she dropped the money onto the ground.

She could smell and taste the stale alcohol on his

lips and the fetid smell of tobacco. She felt that she was suffocating, her head spinning and tears running down her face. The gin that she had consumed started to play with her mind and she thought that she was back on the streets after Robert had thrown her out and she was at the mercy of the two terrifying loathsome sailors again. She heard their voices in her head and the grunting of the men in the doorways with the girls that night. Isabella could feel the man's hand groping up her skirts, pushing her legs apart. With heart racing and head spinning she thought she would surely die and with all her strength she made a tremendous effort to push them away and shouted,

'No! No. Leave me alone.'

'Hey, what's your game? I've given you good money and I want what's owing me. Or do you like it a little rough; is that what's it's all about? Alright then,' he said, as he gave a grab for the terrified girl, who had pressed herself as far into the doorway as she could.

'No, no,' she screamed again.

'Why, you little bitch,' he said as he raised his hand to smash down on her cheek.

Ellen came running over and took the man's hand.

'Ere you come with me, sir. She's new to the game. Let me show you what a real woman can do,' as she lifted her skirt and teased, 'Want a bit 'a this, sir?'

she said as she lured him away from the distraught Isabella and she led the man to the next doorway. Lucy ran to help Isabella, Sophie, who had disobeyed Lucy's orders and crept from the house to follow the girls, raced up to the man and was just about to kick him when Josie reached out and held onto her. Isabella slid to the floor sobbing, holding her head in her hands as her mind in its drunken haze returned to the present time.

'Oh. Lucy I'm so sorry, I'm so sorry. I wanted to do my job, really I did,' she slurred.

Lucy realised that there was no point in trying to persuade or goad her as she was too distraught for any of that, so she said,

'You take Bella back home, Soph. That's what you can do and I'll have words with yer later, you disobedient little bitch. These streets are no place for you at night and yer knows that,' Lucy scolded Sophie.

* * *

Isabella, back in the safety of the room that had become her home, sat at the table and sobbed, her lip rouge smeared across her face.

'Oh, Sophie, what am I to do? I am not good for much, am I? I couldn't even give the man I love a

303

child,' she cried.

'Now, don't cha go blaming yerself, me lovely. Yer not like the u'vers and they shouldn't have expected you to do a thing like that, now should they? So soon an all. It ain't yer fault. We're just have to think of something else,' Sophie soothed. *Maybe I could teach yer how to pick pockets,* she thought.

The next morning, the other girls returned home and Isabella and Sophie found some bread and a piece of cheese for the night-time workers to break their fast upon, although on a good night the girls would often afford themselves some food from their earnings on their way home and Isabella and Sophie would share in the treat, but not today.

As they all sat around the rough battered table Lucy was the first to speak to Isabella. 'Bella, I know yer must be feeling just awful right now, really I do, but we best get it out in the open and talk about last night and what we are gunna do.'

Isabella looked up from her food and caught the eye of Sophie and quickly put a finger to her lips before Sophie had the chance to say anything.

'Lucy, Ellen, Josie, I must apologise for what happened last night. I wanted to work, really I did. It's just that the smell of him and his rough manner reminded me so much of the terrible time when I thought those drunken sailors were going to force themselves upon me and I just fought back. I think instinct took over. I want to be able to make a contribution to my keep as I know that I can't expect you to do all this while I earn nothing in return. I have lain awake for hours and have racked my brains and for the life of me I am at a loss as to what I can do. I am also concerned that I have not heard from my father. I will compose another letter as it is possible that he didn't receive the first and it somehow got lost. I have every intention of pulling my weight until my father comes for me.'

She looked around at the girls who had stopped eating and were looking at her with intensity. She stopped for a moment, trying to gauge the reaction to the deliverance of the speech that she had rehearsed in her mind over and over during the night. She was so afraid that they might throw her into the street as Robert had done all those weeks ago. She knew that the girls had been long-suffering and tolerant with her and so she continued, 'You have all been so patient with me and so very kind. I beg that you will allow me your indulgence for a few more days and I will come up with a solution. I promise.'

As she spoke the final words a shudder took hold of her as she was jolted back to Robert and his declarations of love for her, *I will love you forever, I promise.* She sat at the table with her elbows resting upon it with her hands across her mouth, closed her eyes and whispered a silent prayer to herself. She was totally exhausted and near to fainting. The girls looked from one to the other without speaking, even Sophie had been struck dumb by this heartfelt plea from her Bella.

Lucy raised her eyebrows and tilted her head as she asked the unspoken question of the jury each in turn who were sitting at the table surrounding the accused. Josie and Ellen both nodded in agreement, giving their approval that the poor unfortunate should be given a few more days grace. In truth they were unsure of what action they were to take should they have felt no compassion for her.

'Alright, me girl, yer make sure that yer find yerself some way of income. It don't matter wot yer do just bring something to help out. Maybe Soph can help yer pick a pocket or something. So we'll say no more about it, shall we?'

Isabella looked to the others and managed a hoarse, 'Thank you,' before dissolving into tears.

'Goud girl, yer don't half blub a lot for a young 'un,' Sophie said, imitating her sister's words that were often applied to herself on occasion. This mimicking made all the girls laugh, relieving the tension of the situation and so the table began to take on its usual chatty, giggly morning state of affairs once again.

CHAPTER 25

Clayton House, Berkshire

After the wedding ceremony, Robert and Caroline Bloom were the last to arrive back at Clayton House, to loud cheers and salutations from the guests.

Robert climbed down from the carriage. *My house*, he felt pleased with himself. *At last I am to be owner of all this and more. Lord Robert Wokingham.*

He smiled at his wife of only a few minutes. He felt so elated that as he helped Caroline from the carriage he gave her a passionate kiss, which produced louder applause and cheers from the awaiting crowd. *Thank you, Caroline my love, what a marvellous wedding gift,* he thought smugly.

'Why, Robert, you are eager for our wedding night, are you not?' She laughed.

'You know I am, my darling. Let's get this wedding breakfast over so we can enjoy the rest of the day,' Robert urged. He was tired with pomp and ceremony and wanted to relax now that the knot was tied and he no longer had to be on his best behaviour.

'Darling it is not yet noon, we will be expected to be here with our guests for most of the day. Be patient, my love, it will be worth it.'

Caroline herself would have preferred to be out of the limelight as she was beginning to feel the tired. She could not be sure how many months gone she really was but she thought by now it must be about four, or maybe more.

They were not having a bride tour after the wedding as she felt it would be too much in her condition, so instead they were going to the old dowager house on the edge of the estate, where they were to set up home. Fortunately, with the knowledge of his forthcoming fatherhood, Robert had been compliant.

The meal went well and Caroline felt the stress of the wedding finally disappear. She was a married woman now and her father had forgiven her indiscretion. She was beginning to feel better with her lot and was able to dance with her guests and enjoy herself. *Well, it is my wedding after all, so let's make the most of it,* she thought to herself. At an acceptable hour the couple left in the carriage to retire for their nuptials.

The day had gone according to plan and the

Wokingham family felt a great relief.

'Now is time for merriment, my dear, Lottie.' Lord Wokingham reassured his wife. 'It is time to relax.'

Lady Louisa gave a sigh of relief, 'Thank you, Edward,' she said as she kissed her husband and pulled him close to dance an Allemande with her.

* * *

A few days later Edward invited Robert to come to the house to discuss with him the ships and cargo business they were about to embark upon. Robert informed him that he would have to go back to London, for he had word from Benson that the supply ship that was to accompany the Ivory Rose was now fully stocked with provisions and water, and they were hoping to be ready to weigh anchor soon.

In truth Robert needed to escape from the suffocation of family life. It suited him only in small doses.

He then casually asked the question that had been burning in his thoughts but had not dared to voice until, now lest his true motive for the marriage be discovered.

'Well, Edward, now that I am the Lady Caroline's husband which of the titles can be afforded me at this time? I need to get things right for my arrival back into London society, sir.'

Lord Wokingham had been waiting for this question and was rather surprised that it had taken Robert so long to ask,

'Why, Robert my good fellow. I thought you understood that the title is Caroline's alone, unless you have a title in your own right, which I don't believe you do, sir, or I'm sure you would have mentioned it by now, my good man. I'm afraid it's just plain Mr for you, my friend.'

Robert could not believe what he was hearing. *Can this be true? Have I been that stupid? Why had I not clarified the facts? Something that I never do. Why. I would rip Benson's head off for doing something as foolish. What a total fool I have been. Why hadn't Pringle informed me?* Then Robert remembered that he hadn't given Pringle much time to go over the contracts that day in his office as he was in a hurry to get them ratified and it hadn't occurred to Robert to inquire about a title. He just assumed it to be the case.

He just stared at Edward, his mind racing, trying to gain control of his bitter disappointment. Well, he had all the benefits of the aristocracy. Be sensible man, he told himself. There was a lot of money to be made as well with the business ventures that he and Edward were setting up. So he tried to cover his embarrassment by laughing and saying, 'Oh, of course I realised, but I just wondered if maybe there was a little something.'

'No, Robert, I'm afraid not, old man. Now if that is all I won't keep you from your lovely wife a minute longer. Do come to dinner tonight,' Edward said as he thought, *As soon as I can rid myself of this upstart the better. The widow Bloom could then bring her baby up with the help of her MacGarrett family.*

'Thank you,' Robert said as he hurriedly left the house.

That night he could not sleep. He cursed himself for the lack of thoroughness that had left him untitled; he was usually so meticulous in his attention to detail.

* * *

Robert made his return back to London, leaving his wife, who seemed to be getting bigger by the moment, *to get on with women's work, whatever that was*, he thought to himself. He had been assured by Caroline that her fast-swelling belly was a sure sign that the baby was a healthy one and probably a boy.

CHAPTER 26

Berkeley Street, London

Robert arrived back in London and was eager to get to the wharf, but before leaving the house he had called for Sarah and Bruce to attend him in the drawing room.

'Close the door, Sarah,' he said as he considered his words carefully, 'I know that you had a rather unusual relationship with the last housekeeper that worked here.' Sarah looked up and looked at Robert squarely in the eyes. She didn't hide her face as she would normally have done. She reached out and grabbed Bruce's arm, as if to restrain him, 'Sarah, I know I need not remind you or Bruce of your place,' he said sternly.

Sarah squeezed hard on Bruce's arm by way of a warning to do nothing as she was sure some unpleasant news was about to be relayed.

'I have called you here out of courtesy to inform you that during my stay away I engaged in a marriage with Lady Caroline Wokingham, now Lady Caroline

Bloom, although she maintains the Wokingham title,' Robert felt smug at hearing himself say these words.

'What? You. . . you. . .' Bruce was fortunately stuck for words as Sarah cleverly covered for him.

'What Bruce is trying to say, sir is, what wonderful news you bring us. Congratulations, sir,' she said with a curtsy and quickly tightened her grip on a dumbfounded Bruce as she dragged him out of the room and down the stairs.

They both sat at the table in the kitchen in total shock at the news of the master's marriage. They drank tea from the morning's breakfast, hoping the hot, sweet liquid would help sooth them. Being in a merchant's household had afforded them some secret pleasures.

'Sarah, how could he, the bastard? He must have been planning that all along. That's why he got miss out of the house. What a low life of a man,' Bruce was beside himself with distress.

'Bruce, please stay calm. We knew it was to happen from the letter that we found. I feel the same way as you, but shouting about it won't change a thing. We must keep our heads if we are to keep our positions here. I'm not making light of it but if we were to be dismissed we wouldn't be together. Where would we go, we would be paupers.'

Bruce realised the wisdom of her words and

nodded, 'I know, Sarah, you are always so wise. But that doesn't make me feel any different about the bugger that we work for.'

'No, my little one, but we must keep that to ourselves and be clever. But I do so worry as to what has become of our lovely miss after all this time. You don't think that Billy has found her and done away with her, do you?' Sarah began to fret. It was the usual recurrence most mornings when the two had time to think about Miss Isabella.

Bruce reached out and touched Sarah's hand, 'No, Sarah, we would have had word from Jack by now, I know we would. He would have told us if Billy had done anything with miss. I will go out again today and see if I can find any news of her,' Bruce comforted. 'I know, I'll see if Mrs Barbara has returned from the country, she seems to have been gone a long time. And I bet Miss Isabella is back home with her father and going to all the balls in the big house. Just like this, me lady,' Bruce said as he jumped up from his seat, bowed low from the waist whilst grabbing Sarah by the hand and starting to dance around the kitchen with her.

'Oh, Bruce you are so funny, what would I do without you?' Sarah laughed as she wiped her eyes. For a moment Sarah could smile again but she suddenly stood still with sadness as it dawned on her and she whispered, barely able to speak, 'She would have written, Bruce, you know she would have done.'

Berwick Street, London

Isabella sat with pen in hand trying to compose a more heartfelt plea to her father, in the hope that it would reach him and touch his heart. The last letter must have been mislaid or lost somehow or maybe – Isabella could hardly allow the thoughts to enter her mind – maybe Father didn't forgive me for ruining my only chance to make a good match.

CHAPTER 27

The Morton's House, Bristol

Clara Grey was in her bedchamber, seated in the chair by the window, gazing down on Elizabeth, her sister Jane's daughter, who was cutting some fresh roses in the garden below for the large vase in the sitting room.

Clara's health was failing her quicker than she would have liked and she couldn't muster very much strength these days. Her sister, who was never a strong woman, had passed six years, previously. She had left Clara and Elizabeth well provided for and they lived very comfortably.

Clara had continued to raise the child to the best of her ability with the help of Kate, the wet nurse who had become the housemaid and lady's companion.

As Clara watched Elizabeth her thoughts took hold, as often they did, to the last few days at Brayfield House, before she and Jane went back to live in Bristol. Clara's mind revisited this time with guilt and remorse, more regularly as she surmised she was nearing her final weeks on earth. She felt a nagging urge to put something right before it was too late.

As Elizabeth came in from the garden, she popped some of the flowers into a vase and took them up to her aunt, 'Aunt Clara, here, I thought these roses would cheer you up, they are your favourites. I picked them myself, fresh from the garden,' she said as she placed them on the little table by the chair.

'Thank you, my dear, they are beautiful. Now please sit here next to me as I have something of grave importance to tell you.'

Elizabeth showed worry on her face as she looked at her aunt.

'But the doctor said that you are doing very well, Aunt. It's not about your health, is it?' she said, as she sat down.

'No, my dear, it's not about that. It's about a wrong that I and your mother, God rest her soul, have done to you.'

Elizabeth stretched over and took Clara's hand in hers. She could see the poor woman was distressed.

'A wrong, Aunt, what is it? I don't believe that you or mother would do me any harm.'

Clara didn't know where to begin but tried as best she could, 'Please remember Elizabeth that your mother and I, love you very much and we saw no real harm in what we did. We felt you were a gift from God, as you were… not a child that your mother had actually given birth to, although at one point we were hoping to make this deception ring true. But we had second thoughts, so we told you that we were your guardians after we had found you abandoned on the doorstep in the cold.'

Elizabeth showed some need to move the conversation along as she was getting impatient with concern, 'Yes, Aunt?'

'It all started when I was living and working on the Beaumont's estate in Wessex as a cook, as you well know, and would often have to help out as midwife to the women thereabouts as we all had to take a turn at this, if and when it suited.'

Elizabeth looked at her aunt and frowned, not sure where this conversation was heading.

'Elizabeth, please be patient with me, it not easy to tell you this. When you have heard me out, all will become clear to you.'

'Yes, Aunt, I am sorry, please continue. I will listen quietly,' the young girl reassured the elderly woman.

'Well, the children of the house had a governess, her name was Martha Walker and she was expecting a baby. Her husband was Thomas Walker, the Estate

Manager. Well, when Martha went into labour, I was called upon to help out. I was leaving the employ of the Beaumont's to come to Bristol to live with your mother, who had come to Wessex to stay with me while she was in mourning after the death of her husband, Captain Morton.'

'Yes, I know, he was a good man,' Elizabeth exclaimed.

'Hush, child, do not interrupt. You'll get your say in a minute. Anyway, as I was leaving the estate, I had to train my successor Alice Price to be the cook and make sure that she was also competent with birthing of babies once I had left, so she accompanied me. Well, it had been a long labour with much pain, sweat and hard work and we were all very tired, then at last Martha's child was born. I gathered the child up while Alice wiped the exhausted mother down, but the baby made no sound and lay lifeless in my arms.'

Elizabeth gave a gasp.

'I tried every trick I knew, but try as I might I could not get the baby to respond and so found it to be dead and not wanting to distress Martha at this stage I quickly wrapped the little mite up into a sheet and instructed Alice to take it and place it on a shelf in the cold room. I told her that she was to hurry back to help deliver the after birth. Alice did this as quickly as she could. She was not used to the wonders of childbirth, her ears had only ever heard about it, but now her eyes had seen.'

Elizabeth sat quite still wondering how this could affect her but she was resigned to hearing the story out.

'Well, whilst Alice was out of the room, Martha had further pains and lo and behold another baby was on its way into the world. Well, I couldn't believe my eyes and I prayed that this second baby would be alive this time. Alice re-entered the bedchamber just in time to see the second baby being born. I quickly wiped away the white sludge and blood from the infant, and it began to cry. I was so happy this child had survived and I handed the baby to be suckled to a rather exhausted mother. "There you are, my dear, a beautiful little girl," I said to Martha, who managed a contented smile and said, "Isabella. My baby is Isabella."

Clara's mind drifted further and she remembered how she had congratulated Martha and Thomas, her husband, who had been called to his wife's side once the baby had been born.

'I did not want to cause upset to the new parents by telling them that they had had a stillborn baby as well, so I whispered to Alice that she was never to mention the stillborn as this would serve no purpose, it would only distress the new mother and father and take away the joy of celebrating their new baby daughter.

Alice realised that Martha, in her labour delirium, did not know that in fact two babies had been born of her and it was better for all that it was left that way. Alice told me she understood and that no one would hear it from her lips.'

Elizabeth was showing more attention.

'Once I was satisfied that all was well with Martha and the new baby, I bade them farewell and readied myself to make my way home. I was exhausted and tired from all the work, it's not called labour for nothing, but first I had to stop off at the cold room to collect the stillborn. I needed to get back to my cottage and seal it in a burial sack, so that I could take it to be buried the next day, behind the church which was set aside for the unfortunates of the village that were delivered, but without name, or ceremony. I was hurrying back to my cottage. I had a lantern in one hand and I was clutching the stillborn inside my cloak in the other. As I walked in the cold still of the night I had to hold the baby tight, lest I dropped it, for although it was dead I still treated it with the respect that it deserved. Then, Elizabeth, for one moment I thought that I felt it move. "No, don't be silly," I told myself and I pressed the child even closer to me as I thought that I had felt that the movement was actually the baby slipping from my grasp. I was almost home when there it was again a definite movement accompanied this time with a little whimper. "What is this," I thought as I urgently opened my door and moved swiftly into the kitchen. I placed the bundle on the table and unwrapped the cloth around it. My heart was pounding. I pulled at the sheet until at last I was staring into the beautiful eyes of a living baby girl.'

Elizabeth gasped again in wonderment and was getting rather excited.

'I called to my sister Jane to come quickly. "What is it, Clara?" she said. "Here, look," I said, "look at Martha's baby." I then told your mother all that had happened that night. "Oh, Clara, she is so beautiful. Look at her. She is so lovely," your mother said and scooped the baby up into her arms and held her close. "You can't take her back this time of night. Here, let me comfort her," she said to me.'

Clara felt exhausted from the emotion and effort of telling the story and she asked Elizabeth to fetch her a glass of water so that she may continue. Once refreshed Clara picked up the story again. 'Your mother was right, I couldn't take the baby back on such a cold night. "But," I said, "first thing in the morning I must take her back. In the meantime we must give her some cooled boiled water to sustain her."

"Thank you, Clara," Jane had said and she carried the baby to her bedchamber and I heard her say to the infant, "I think we will call you Elizabeth." Clara paused for a moment.

'Elizabeth. But that's my name,' Elizabeth exclaimed.

'Well, your mother took Elizabeth upstairs with her.' Clara took another sip from her glass of water. 'Next morning, when I came down the stairs, I found that the drapes had been pulled open around the window and the window was open to allow a little air to circulate around the little cottage. I found Jane humming as she sat in a chair cradling the baby. It appeared that Jane had been awake for several hours and had cleaned the cottage. It was spick and span and gleaming, something that had not happened in a long time as Jane, your mother, had spent most days lain in bed, too distraught from the loss of her husband. And more over from the loss of the baby that she herself had been carrying until the day her husband died. She had been six months with child when the miscarriage happened, a second blow that took her into the realms of grief, after which she didn't give much care to the world.

Now she was quite changed. She had gone from the grieving widow and was almost back to her old self.

Even the baby was gurgling contentedly. She bade me good morning and informed me that she and Elizabeth had slept well as she gave the baby a kiss on the head. I was in no rush to get back to the big house as, fortunately, Alice had taken over most of my duties now and I knew that my presence would not be missed. I turned to your mother and urged that I had to take the baby back that morning. I told her as gently as I could as I could see she was already very attached to the baby. The love shone from her eyes.' Clara stopped talking again, feeling that she could not go on with the rest of the story.

'Please, Aunt, pray continue,' Elizabeth urged.

'Your mother was beside herself saying, "No, sister, no you can't take Elizabeth away. Please, sister, please help me. I love this little baby. It was meant to be," your mother pleaded with me to let her keep the baby. But the baby is not yours to keep, I told her. She belongs to Martha and Thomas, you know that.'

Clara told the story with tear-filled eyes, but she pressed on, 'Your mother placed the baby in a little drawer she had lined with a blanket and it made a perfect little crib. "Please, Clara," she said again, "please let us keep Elizabeth. We can give her a good home, she will be well provided for." Your mother wept on her knees, clinging to my skirts. "Please, Clara,

325

please help me. I haven't lost my senses, far from it. We will be so happy now. I can be Elizabeth's mother and you will be Auntie Clara. We can raise her together in Bristol, no one will know," your mother reassured me.'

Elizabeth had a frowned look on her face as she was putting the facts of this conversation together and was terrified to hear the rest. Clara saw this look but had come too far to turn back now.

"'Jane," I said, "we can't, it is nothing short of stealing, no worse, "Kidnapping." We just can't do it." Your mother begged me again, "I will not be able to have a child of my own, the Captain and I dearly wanted one and it took years to happen. Please, Clara. Martha has another child and by all accounts, she was unaware that she had been delivered of two, being under the influence of the pain draught you gave her. Please, Clara. Please." Jane's weeping was so pitiful that I was torn in two. I dearly loved my only sister and I could see the joy that baby Elizabeth was bringing to her. I sat and gave it a lot of thought. I closed my eyes and I felt my breathing become difficult. What was I to do? "Jane, you know we will be committing a crime, don't you?" I asked her and she nodded her head. "No one must ever find out or we will be in the trouble of the worst kind. Are you prepared for that?" I asked.

Jane ran to me and held me. "Oh, yes, Clara, yes. Thank you so much. I don't think you know what this means to me," she said. But of course I did or I wouldn't have agreed to such a thing.'

Clara hurried on with what must come out into the open, although she was sure that Elizabeth had guessed the truth already but Clara wanted to get to the end before she could be interrupted, 'I had to think quickly and practically for the baby's sake as Elizabeth needed feeding. I knew of a girl, her name was Kate.'

At this point Elizabeth was sure that what she was dreading was true.

'She lived on the edge of the village, she had lost her baby and her husband several months ago in a fire. She had no one hereabouts and to make a living she hired herself out as a wet nurse. I didn't know her very well but I did feel sorry for her. I had the idea that might suit all of us very well. When your mother came to stay with me no one saw her as she had hidden herself away in her grief. So fortunately, no one could possibly know how far gone she was with child or without. So I told her that she must let people think that I delivered her baby last night. "I delivered your baby. Your baby Elizabeth, last night," I told her. "Do you understand me?" I said, "'Yes," she confirmed that she understood. I hurried off to find Kate and I asked her if she would come and wet nurse Elizabeth and ask if she would come to live with us down here in Bristol. Fortunately, Kate, who you now know very well, agreed.'

'Kate? Our Kate, who lives here you mean?' Although, Elizabeth had realised the situation she needed to hear it said so as to be true. She sat and stared at her aunt.

'Yes, our Kate. Well, there you have it, Elizabeth. I know that you have worked it all out for yourself. Now you know your real mother's name was Martha, you have always known that I am not your real aunt, but we love you as much as any family could, if not more. You are very, very cherished. Please forgive two desperate women. You have made our lives so special and I know that I could speak for your mother, er. . . your mother Jane, that is. I hope that we have made your life special too. I am, so, so sorry, my darling, this must be a shock and some devastating news for you, but I couldn't leave this world with you not knowing the truth. You were not left on any doorstep, you are not an unknown. Your real name is Elizabeth Walker. Your real mother is Martha and your father is Thomas.'

Elizabeth sat quite still, in total shock.

'I need a moment to digest this,' she said and fled out of the room and down the stairs and sat on the bench in the garden. She sat and she stared, for what amounted to almost an hour, running over and over in her head what she had just heard, until finally the tears began to flow. *So where is Martha, my mother? And where is my father?* The questions came rushing into her mind. Then she realised that her aunt had told her that there was another baby, Isabella. *I am a twin, I have a twin sister.* She ran back upstairs to put a thousand questions to her aunt.

Elizabeth entered her aunt's bedchamber, 'Aunt Clara, there is so much that I have to say to you and ask you,' she said quite solemnly.

Clara turned and gestured for Elizabeth to sit by her side, 'Yes, Elizabeth, my heart goes out to you and I am sorry that I have had to put you through all this. I wanted to tell you when your mother, your mother Jane, that is, passed away but I couldn't find the words. I am so sorry, my darling,' Clara said as she reached for her handkerchief to wipe the tears of sadness from her tired old eyes. 'I wouldn't hurt you for the world and now I fear I have lost your love forever,' she said.

'No, Aunt, I still love you and the memory of my mother. I don't want to make a quick judgement. You have always taught me not to judge, as we all do things we believe are right at the time and although you both knew it to be wrong, I do realise your desperation must have been so great to make you do such a thing. I am no longer a child and must not act as one.'

'Oh, Elizabeth, you are wise beyond your years. Can you forgive me and your Mother?' Clara said as she wiped more tears from her eyes.

'My dearest Aunt, you are both forgiven. I love you both very much. You have brought me up well, I have been very happy and wanted for nothing. I have had a good childhood and education. But I must find out about my other family. Martha, Thomas and of course my sister, Isabella. Please tell me all you know, Aunt. Just because I want to go and search for them doesn't mean I love you less; I just have a longing to know the other part of me.'

'Elizabeth, my darling, I will tell you all that I know, but to be honest it is not much more than I have already told you. It was a long time ago now.'

Clara spoke and relived her life at Brayfield House.

'Thank you, Aunt. I will leave for Wessex soon so that I may get to know my other family. It will be a shock to them as well, I am sure. Do you think that I will look like my sister?' Elizabeth asked.

'Well, you are twins so I imagine it's a good possibility. If it helps, you are the image of your mother Martha, you really are. At times I have found your resemblance difficult to live with, as it reminds me of what we have done.' A tear trickled down Clara's cheek at this thought.

ℰℭ

TO BE CONTINUED IN
BEYOND REDEMPTION
Book Two

ℰℭ

Printed in Great Britain
by Amazon

43222251R00187